THE GOLDEN GOD

THE ARES TRIALS

ELIZA RAINE
ROSE WILSON

Editors: Christopher Mitchell

Cover: Yocla Designs

ELIZA RAINE
ROSE WILSON

BOOK THREE
— OF THE —
ARES TRIALS

For all those who feel they don't belong.
Your tribe is out there.

1

BELLA

"Where are we going?"

Freezing air raced over my skin as Dentro soared through the sky, my body still clutched in the grip of his bark-covered tail. I could feel the dragon's pleasure rolling from him, his aura blissful as his huge wings stretched out, slicing through the clouds.

He was free.

I, on the other hand, couldn't have felt less free.

I was broken, trapped in an agony I had never felt the likes of in my pain-filled life.

The tears had stopped, but the rage and sorrow had only grown. My chest physically hurt, as though lumps of my insides had been ripped out, and all that was left was a hollow despair that ached worse than any wound I'd ever experienced.

I'd been so close to a contentment I had never even dared to dream of reaching.

Love.

Ares had said he loved me. Nobody had ever loved me. Hell, *I* hadn't even loved me for most of my life.

But Ares did. And I loved him. We were right, somehow. Not because we were the same, but because we weren't. Our differences were what made us fit together so perfectly.

We shared the same fierce desire for violence, confrontation and victory, but we could teach each other so much about how to handle it.

And gods, we could fight well together. There was no doubt in my mind that we could love each other with the same intensity. The thought of being in Ares' arms, our love for each other in every touch, made the acid feeling in my chest spread painfully.

Aphrodite had ruined everything. The jealous, spiteful, cruel goddess had sent him mad with battle-lust, just so I could see how savage he could be. Did she think that would scare me off?

The woman was a fucking idiot. I shared Ares' power. I *knew* how savage he could be. I had the same damn temper, the same violence within me. She didn't need to show me.

I already knew that Ares could control the beast of War, so what he buried inside himself meant nothing to me. I only cared how he *chose* to live his life. His actions were what mattered, not how destructive he had the potential to become. Hell, if I were to be judged on my own potential savageness, I would fare no better than the God of War.

The memory of him lifting his monstrous foot to slam down on my helpless body speared through me. I didn't hate him for draining my power and trying to kill me. It wasn't really him. But hearing his cold words on repeat in my head was torture. It reminded me constantly of how painful the loss of his love was, and how brutally his passion had been ripped away from me.

The dragon banked, snapping my focus down below us. A sparkling blue ocean glittered around a large island in the distance. I could make out lots of forestland, and towns of gleaming white buildings dotting the cliffs. Piers jutted out over the water in several places, and massive ships were docked at them, their solar sails shining.

"This is Hera's realm." Dentro's voice sounded in my mind.

"Hera?"

"Yes. You, fierce one, have a love curse to break. And the only other goddess who specializes in love is Hera."

"But nobody has seen her since Zeus vanished."

"Ares is her son," Dentro said, his wise voice gentle. *"She will see you."*

Hope mingled with fear. "What if she won't? Ares said parents don't care about their kids in Olympus."

"Hera will see you. A bond such as the one you share with Ares runs deep enough that she will be aware of it."

I remembered what Eris had said about Hera's unbreakable marriage bonds between Gods. Last time, the thought had alarmed me. This time, I clung to the notion that something still connected me to the God of War. "I thought you had to consent to Hera's bonds?"

"You do."

"I've never consented to anything like that."

"Not that you are aware of. I believe that there is much you are not aware of."

A sick feeling made my already roiling stomach clench. If Hera really was going to see me, then I would refuse to leave until I got some answers. I was done letting others tell me that there was all this damn mystery about my past that they all suspected, and only I didn't seem to know.

The dragon tilted so that we flew faster toward the center of the island, where the forest was at its thickest. *"Call to Hera,"* he instructed.

"How?"

"Picture her in your mind."

"I don't know what she looks like."

Dentro let out a snort, and whether it was from annoyance or surprise, I wasn't sure. He began to vibrate, and I gripped his tail tight. Then, with a flash of teal light, an enormous marble column burst up from the trees below us. It rose higher, the carved swirls decorating its perfectly Greek looking top.

The column slowed to a stop thirty feet above the forest, then the air shimmered as a temple took shape before my eyes, fitting atop the column exactly. It was beautiful, with carved columns holding up a triangular facade at the front, and an impressive number of steps leading to grand wooden doors. Grapes were carved all over the marble, I saw as we got closer, and I could also make out lots of images of crabs and peacocks.

The dragon swooped lower and lower, until we were in front of the steps, facing the imposing doors that led inside the temple. My mind darted immediately back to the last staircase I had ascended - the one that could have killed me and Ares in Panic's tower. The one we had beaten together, our lust for each other burning through our bodies as we conquered our challenge.

Dentro set me down carefully on the marble and my bare feet throbbed as they met the cold stone, but only for a moment. I was still wearing the gown, though the skirts were torn and muddied. *Ischyros* was pulsing, warm and comforting in my hand. The dragon's head moved low, so that one huge eye was level with my face.

"Good luck. I will be waiting here," he said aloud, his voice musical and rumbling.

"Thank you," I said. "For saving me, I mean. Ares would have killed me."

"I owed you."

"Well, now the debt is clear. I don't want you beholden to me. You're free now."

"I will not be waiting here for you because I am obligated to, fierce one. I will be waiting because I like you." Amusement gleamed in his green eye, and a tiny piece of my shattered chest seemed to heal a little. I had a friend.

"I like you too," I said, not quite able to summon a smile, but projecting my sincerity into the words.

"Good. I have a feeling that you will need this."

Dentro's tail snaked round, and he deposited the helmet that we had stolen from Panic's treasure room at my feet.

"You took it?" I stared in surprise.

"I believe it is important."

"Why? Do you know where it came from?"

"No. But it emanates the same power that you do."

"War magic?"

"No. *Bella* magic."

I blinked up at the dragon. "Bella magic," I repeated on a breath. I liked the sound of that. I bent, scooping it up. My heart fluttered as I saw how damaged it was. It must have born the brunt of Ares' stamping feet, because the metal was completely caved in on one side, and it would have been impossible to wear.

"It can't have been that strong if it was crushed so easily," I said, trying to hide my disappointment. Ares' armor was indestructible.

"Keep it with you none-the-less," Dentro said. "Now, go."

I nodded, and squared my shoulders. *Ischyros* hummed again in my hand, pumping confidence through me. It was time to meet the Queen of the Olympians.

2

BELLA

The silence that dominated the temple wasn't oppressive or heavy. It was oddly peaceful, compared to the turmoil churning through me. The huge doors had opened of their own accord as soon as I had approached them and a long pool ran all the way down the middle of the expansive space that was revealed. The water that filled it was a joyful, vibrant turquoise and I wanted to run my fingers through it as I walked alongside it. Peacocks roamed the marble floors, moving between the mammoth columns holding up the roof. My gaze followed the columns up, where long slats had been carved from the stone, allowing in the shafts of bright light that illuminated the temple. At the far end of the space, presiding over the pool, was an enormous gold statue of a handsome woman, a proud set to her unsmiling mouth, and wisdom in her intricately sculpted eyes. She wore a toga and a large crown, with vicious spikes that were interspersed with peacock feathers.

It was Hera. I knew the instant I saw it.

"Bella." A deep female voice rang through the temple, and the statue shimmered with teal light.

I dropped to one knee without thought. "My Queen," I answered, the words springing to my lips, unbidden. But I wasn't being forced to say them. I frowned as I straightened. It was more like muscle-memory, something that I had done for so long that I knew to do it.

"You are remembering."

"Remembering what?"

"You were not born of the mortal world. You know that. You have many long-suppressed memories of Olympus."

"Where are you?" I spun, looking for any sign of movement that wasn't a damn peacock.

"I regret that I cannot be with you. I have a task that is occupying all of my time. And strength." She added the last two words in a rueful tone.

I longed to ask her what she meant, but I had questions that were much more important.

"How do I break Ares' curse?"

"I am pleased you are asking me this." There was a note of approval in her voice. "You must visit with Hephaestus. Aphrodite is his wife, and he knows more about her magic than I, or anyone else, does."

I felt my eyebrows jump up in surprise. "You want me to go see Aphrodite's husband? Surely he would hate Ares? Why would he want to help him?"

"It is not our place to judge the relationships of

others. How Aphrodite and Hephaestus conduct their marriage is their business."

I frowned, feeling slightly chastised. "Oh." I swallowed, then asked the question burning on my lips. "Hera, am I bound to Ares?"

There was a long pause before she answered. "You know that you are. You feel it."

"Were we bound by you? Is this one of the memories I have lost?"

"No. You were bound by powers beyond my control. And in more than one way. The connection that allows you to share your power is physical, contained by distance. You can only share your magic when you are in each other's company." I nodded. I knew that was true, and it was how Dentro had saved me from Ares' bloodlust. He'd taken me far enough away that Ares couldn't draw my magic from me. "That connection comes from the War power that you share, and is not unheard of. It is similar to how Ares shares his powers with the Lords. But the bond between your souls is different. It is the same as the connection that I am able to create between lovers. Once brought to life by mutual love, it will allow you to feel each other over any distance, and know if the other is happy, sad, or angry. And you will never, ever be whole again without it. I don't know how you two were fated in such a way, but I have done what I can for my son to find you. To find happiness. He may not know, or believe that, but it is true."

"Tell me who I am, how I ended up in the mortal world?" I couldn't stop the words tumbling from me.

"Just as you are bound to Ares, I am bound to prophecy. You must find your own way to your truth." I bit down on the surge of anger I felt at her answer. She was no more helpful than Zeeva. "Oh Enyo, I am so much more helpful than Zeeva."

I hissed, slamming up a defensive wall around my thoughts. "That's not fair," I said, before I could stop myself.

"You are a visitor here, in my temple. Your thoughts in this place belong to me." Her voice was hard and filled with power. I felt my knees weaken and gripped my sword, pulling on its strength.

"Can you tell me anything else?" I asked, through gritted teeth.

"My absence from Olympus is not for nothing. Contrary to what many believe, my husband is worth saving. And I will stop at nothing to do so."

"I can respect that," I nodded. Even though Zeus sounded like a total fuckwad. I was careful to guard that thought.

A rumbling flickered through the stone, and Hera spoke again. "Visit Hephaestus. Take that helmet with you. And... help my son."

There was another shimmer of light over the statue, and the unearthly presence of the goddess vanished.

"Bella." I looked down, startled at the voice, and a rush of relief powered through my tense body.

"Zeeva."

The cat blinked slowly at me. *"I am glad to see you safe."*

"Really?"

"Why do you sound surprised?"

I cocked my head at her. "Because you're never there when I need you? Because you only show up after all the bad shit has happened?"

Zeeva swished her tail. *"You know I can only help you from a distance. I was in the forest when Ares changed."*

"You were?"

"Yes. And if Dentro had not arrived, I would have helped you. My duties and bonds make it hard for me to involve myself, but I would have sought help before Ares could kill you." Something warm stirred in my chest at the sincerity I could hear in her normally cool voice.

Maybe I had two friends. They may be a dragon and a sphinx-shifter but I'd take that over two humans any day of the week.

"Do you know how to get to Hephaestus?" I asked her.

"Yes. And so will Dentro."

"Good. The sooner we get back to Ares, the better."

3

BELLA

We flew for a long time, and as we did Zeeva talked me through the basics of flashing. There was no question it was something I needed to learn, and I focused on her words intently, pouring my frazzled energy into the task of learning. Anything to stop the memory of those cold, emotionless eyes in the face of the man I loved.

Flashing was dangerous, Zeeva said. If done incorrectly I could end up separated from my soul. I refrained from telling her that my distance from Ares right now already felt like I had been separated from my soul. I didn't understand the depth of my feelings for the god, or how someone as practical and wary as I usually was could feel so passionately about a man I'd known for such little time. But Hera's words played in my head, warring with Zeeva's for my attention.

"You were bound by powers beyond my control. Just as you are bound to Ares, I am bound to prophecy. You must find your own way to your truth."

What did that even mean? Who the hell got involved with my life before I could even remember and bound me to Ares? And why? What the fuck did prophecy have to do with it?

Ares would have to tell me. I had no doubt he knew more than he had told me so far, and now that he had professed his love for me...

His giant foot stamping down toward me as his savage bellow echoed through the forest flooded my memory. I squeezed my eyes shut, realizing that Zeeva's voice had fallen quiet.

"Do you fear him?" she asked gently.

My eyes fluttered open as I shook my head hard. I was wrapped in Dentro's tail again, and Zeeva was sat on the bark a foot or so from me, her magically enhanced claws set deep into the wood to keep her balance. Dentro had assured us that his skin was thick enough to take it. Pastel pink and orange clouds whooshed by on either side of us, cool air flowing through my hair.

"I don't fear him. I know he would have killed me, but I'm not scared of what's inside him. He was forced to lose control, by another god. There's nothing wrong with his own control."

Light sparked in Zeeva's amber eyes. *"And control is what is important to you?"*

"Of course it is. We are nothing past the decisions we make. I've spent my life making choices to contain my destruction."

"And you agree with the choices Ares has made?"

"Not all of them. But he is not cruel, or unnecessarily violent, which his power could easily make him. He is arrogant and egotistical, but I think I would be too if I were an Olympian god."

"I hope, very much, that you two can be together." The cat's voice was gentler than I had ever heard it, and I cocked my head in question at her. *"It is rare to see such understanding of a person's darker traits. Such optimism could transform a life. Many lives."*

"It's not hard to understand him. I share his power. Hera said... She said I was bound to him, but not by her. Do you know what that means?"

"No. I don't. I knew that you were connected, and that Hera has a great deal of interest in you two. But no more."

"Do you know how I can get my memories back?" At the question, Zeeva dropped her gaze.

"I can give some of them to you."

My heart skipped a beat as I stared at Zeeva. "What?"

She looked back at me. *"I have been with you for much longer than you know. And I can return some of your memories to you. But not here and now. You need space, and a clear mind."*

For once, I did not argue with her. Concentrating on getting Ares back was more important. And, if I was being honest, a part of me was a little afraid of my own past. What if I didn't like what I remembered? And I had no doubt that I would end up with a whole new set of questions that I didn't have the answers to. I wasn't quite ready for that.

"Why were my memories taken?"

"We will discuss it later."

"OK. What is taking all of Hera's time and strength?"

"That's my Queen's business," Zeeva said, formal once again.

"Fine." I shifted in Dentro's tail, my magical barrier against his scratchy bark now second-nature to me. I didn't even have to think about it to keep it in place. I reached for the well of power inside me, finding it hotter and larger than it had ever been before. My strength now that I was away from Ares was huge.

"Tell me again about the flashing. I have to picture where I want to go? What if I don't know what it looks like?"

Zeeva seemed relieved to answer my question, and as we settled back into the lesson, I tried my hardest to use my ability for laser-focus to concentrate on her words and ignore my gut-wrenching awareness of Ares' absence.

"Dragon?"

A booming, throaty voice filled the sky around us, and my body fired to life as I jerked awake. "What -" My question was cut off as Dentro answered the voice.

"Mighty Hephaestus. It has been a long time."

I blinked rapidly, trying to expel the sleep from my brain. My neck was sore, and my shoulders ached, but I leaned over the tail wrapped around me to peer down. The peaks of three volcanoes were rising majestically from the ocean, and I could see the bright molten lava in each of them. Excitement fizzed through me. We had arrived in Hephaestus' realm, Scorpio.

"Hera warned me of your arrival." The god's voice was deep and clipped, and not remotely friendly. "Will you wait here, Dentro?"

"If you do not mind. The inside of a volcano is a dangerous place for a being made of wood." There was an amusement to Dentro's voice as he answered, and I felt my eyes widen.

"The inside of a volcano?" I hissed at Zeeva. She just blinked slowly at me.

The very tip of Dentro's tail curled up toward me, and he deposited the crushed helmet in my hands. I had tucked *Ischyros*, back in flick-knife mode, inside my bodice when I had realized sleep was going to take me.

"Good luck, fierce one," the dragon said, and then the world flashed white.

4

BELLA

The first thing I was aware of was heat. Serious heat. I looked around myself, feeling naked without my sword and clutching the helmet tightly instead.

I was, indeed, inside a volcano. And it was even more surreal than the flying ship had been.

The only light was coming from a river of blazing orange that bubbled before me. I was standing on dark rock, almost black in color, and I was definitely at the bottom of the epic structure. My neck strained as I looked up. There were rings of rocky platforms lining the inside, and roughly hewn stairways carved into the body of the volcano to connect them. Bridges jutted out at various points, connecting the platforms where there were no stairs and there were waterfalls of eye-wateringly bright lava flowing from huge pools on each floor all the way down to the river in front of me. The sense of being utterly dwarfed engulfed me.

I could only make out details on the first few floors

above me, but I could see enough to work out what was causing the ringing, metallic bangs and thuds that were echoing through the volcano.

Giants. Huge shirtless men stood by the pools of lava, dipping pieces of metal into them, then wielding massive hammers and pokers as they worked at long rocky tables.

Hephaestus was the god of blacksmiths, and this must be his forge. I let out a long, awed breath, aware again of how hot I was as sweat trickled down my neck. The smell of sulfur was strong, and I pulled on my power to lessen it.

"Hello?" I called, hesitantly. The top of the volcano was dark, no light from the sky above shining through. A distinctly claustrophobic feeling edged over me, the desire for fresh air suddenly pervasive.

"Bella," said a voice, then a dark figure appeared at the edge of the platform above me. The figure leaped suddenly, and my mouth fell open as it easily cleared the river of lava, thudding down onto the rock just feet away from me.

I dropped to one knee instinctively, as I took in the features of Hephaestus. His face was hard and cold, his features not quite where they would be on other faces. One of his shoulders was hunched high, making him lopsided, and his black toga was covered by a heavy leather apron. A massive war-hammer swung from his right hand as he considered me.

"Hera said you would be able to help me," I said, as deferentially as I could. I needed this god's help. *Ares* needed this god's help.

"You have upset my wife." I nodded, awkwardly. Hephaestus swung the hammer between his huge hands. "She has been toying with the God of War for too long. Her pride turns her into a fool." His words were rough, as though he needed to clear his throat, and his eyes gave away no emotion.

I swallowed, wishing to hell that there was any kind of breeze in the stifling volcano. "How do I break one of her curses?"

"She is the Goddess of Love. Her curses can only be forged and broken with love."

I blinked. "Loving Ares is what caused the curse," I said. "How can loving him break it?"

Hephaestus narrowed his eyes, then they dropped to the helmet in my hands. Interest flickered in his irises, the light of the lava reflecting in the black orbs. "You understand that my wife loves many men?" he said, after an uncomfortably long pause.

"Erm," I said, not having a freaking clue what to say to that.

"Love is the most powerful thing in the world." The god's voice lowered, and a melancholy crept into his words. "All power has to have balance. No immortal is a force for good, or bad. They must all be both. With the greatest love comes the greatest pain. And with the greatest power comes the greatest wrath. My wife must carry that burden." His eyes locked on mine. "You and I will never know the extent of her hardship."

I bit down on my tongue. I understood his words, and a part of me accepted them. They were not a million miles from what I had said to Zeeva just hours before, about Ares.

But there was another part of me that could never understand or forgive the woman who had attacked the man I loved and stripped him of his self-control due to pure jealousy. Every time I had spoken with her, I had seen the cruelty within her, shining from those beautiful eyes. I knew how she had treated Ares before; like a toy, a pet, a trophy. Perhaps Hephaestus was right and it came as part of the package, being the Goddess of Love. But that didn't mean she had to act on it.

"I do not resent the God of War," Hephaestus said, letting out a sigh and mercifully saving me from saying something I would regret. "But I relish the chance to remove him from my wife's life. What were the words of her curse?"

I wracked my brain, trying to recall Aphrodite's exact words. "She said love made her power work, then she made Ares crazy with blood-lust. He tried to take all of my power by killing me. She told him, *'if you truly love her, and you want her to love you back, she must see you at your worst'.*"

Hephaestus nodded. "You must accept him at his worst. If you still love him, the curse will be broken."

"But I do accept him," I said. "Isn't that enough?" Doubt crept over me. What if I thought I did, but on some subconscious level I didn't?

But... That wasn't possible - I knew how I felt. I loved him.

"Ares needs to know that. It must be mutual. He must see that you accept him at his worst."

"How? If I go near him he'll take my power and kill me."

Hephaestus considered me for a long moment. "Do you still believe that you can prove yourself worthy of Olympus?"

"Still?" I blinked at him, trying to ignore the heat pressing in on me. "I don't know what you mean."

The God of Blacksmiths lifted his hammer. "I will rephrase the question. Are you worthy of Olympus? Of the love of an Olympian?"

"I don't know," I said, staring at Hephaestus. I had no idea what was necessary to be worthy of Olympus. If it meant acting like Aphrodite, then no - I wasn't. And as for being worthy of Ares... "All I know is that I love him. I'll do whatever it takes to save him. Whatever is needed for him to know how I feel."

"I will help you, but you will have to earn it."

Relief washed through me. "I'll do anything."

Hephaestus held out his hand, dropping his hammer to the rock with a crack. "Give me that," he said, pointing at the crushed helmet in my hands.

I stepped forward, placing it tentatively into his enormous outstretched hand. "I made this for you many years ago," he said quietly. "I didn't know that it was you I was welding it for, at the time."

Excitement flared inside me. "Really?"

"Indeed. I make many things for the Olympians." My skin prickled with goosebumps, despite the suffocating heat.

"I'm no Olympian."

"No. You are not." He looked from the helmet to me.

"If you can gather what I need from my realm to repair the helmet, then you will be able to break the curse and save Ares."

"How?"

"When you wear this helmet, no god will be able to penetrate it," he said, and took a lop-sided stride toward me. My breath caught in my pounding chest.

"Impervious armor? Like Ares has?"

He nodded. "Yes. But Ares' armor protects his body. This helmet is different. It will protect everything internal to you. Your body will be just as susceptible to external influence as it was before, but as long as you are wearing the helmet, your mind, your soul and your power will be guarded."

Understanding smashed into me, the meaning of his words sounding too good to be true. "Ares can't take my power if I'm wearing the helmet?"

"He can not."

"Thank you," I breathed, feeling just a smidgen of the tension wracking my body lessen. "Thank you so much."

"Do not thank me yet. My realm is not an easy place to navigate, and you will need to converse with my general. He is not accustomed to visitors."

"Your general? What do I need to do?"

"You understand that this is a test? Of your worthiness?" I nodded. I had enough brute strength and sheer determination burning through my veins that I was sure I could complete any damn test. "I need a bar of gold and a purple phoenix feather." He held up the helmet, tiny in his palm. "Then I will be able to fix this and you can return to Ares."

"I'm ready. Where do I find them?"

"There are many volcanoes in Scorpio. You will need this to enter one." A black orb shimmered into existence at my feet, the size of a large pebble. I crouched and scooped it up. "If you manage to get both items, you'll be flashed back here."

Before I could answer him, he flashed me out of his volcano without a word of warning.

5

BELLA

"Shit!"

I was falling through the air, the crystal clear ocean fast approaching and the black orb clutched in my hand. I ran through my options lightning fast in my head, and deciding I wasn't confident enough to try and flash myself, braced for impact.

I slammed into the water, feeling as though I'd hit a brick wall before sinking under the surface. I scrambled to kick myself up, refusing to let go of the orb and my skirt tangling around my legs as I tried to swim. A dark shadow moved over me and then I was aware of something dipping into the water next to me. Dentro's tail wrapped around my middle and pulled me from the ocean.

"Bastard, asshole, fuckwit god," I spat, trying to push my wet hair out of my face with one hand, still unwilling to relinquish my grip on the orb.

Dentro chuckled. "He's not known for his hospitality. This realm is forbidden. Most who enter it are killed instantly." The dragon moved me so that I was level with his face, his eyes serious. Zeeva trotted along his snake-like body, stopping and staring at me. Cooling ocean spray combined with the breeze caused by the beating of Dentro's wings, and I took a second to revel in the feeling of cool freedom.

"*Where is the helmet?*" Zeeva asked. "*And what is that?*" She sniffed at the orb.

"If I can find some gold and some purple phoenix feathers, then he'll fix the helmet," I said, hope and excitement rushing through me. "And then it will protect my power. Nobody can get to me when I'm wearing it."

"*Including Ares?*"

"Yes. I'll be able to go back to him." A sense of purpose was replacing the crushing sense of loss, and I felt my power focusing, doubt and grief forced into a backseat.

"Good. Where will you find these things you need?" Dentro asked.

"Erm..." I held up the orb. "All I know is that they're in his realm and I need this."

"Hmmm," The dragon mused, beating his wings and rising above the sea. "All of Scorpio is within volcanoes. I suppose the orb shows you which one you need to visit."

"It's a good job you're here, Dentro," I said, peering closely at the orb as we rose higher. "I would've been here a week working that out."

The orb was rough, and I could make out a pattern on the black stone.

"Look down. There is Scorpio. Does that help?"

I did as the dragon said, seeing a spattering of volcano tips rising form the ocean. There were at least twenty. I scowled. How was I supposed to single out two of them?

It took another five minutes of hovering over Scorpio and Zeeva asking repeatedly for the exact words Hephaestus had said, before I realized what the pattern on the orb was.

"Dentro, move around until that big volcano there is on our right," I said excitedly, holding up the orb. The dragon soared through the sky, moving to where I'd asked him, and I fist pumped the air as the pattern on the orb lined up with the peaks jutting out the ocean below us.

"That's it! The pattern on the rock is a map of the volcanoes! Look!"

Zeeva flicked her tail as she looked at where I was pointing. "Well done."

"Thanks," I said, inspecting the orb. "One of them must be the one we want..." I ran my finger over the little bumps that matched up with the volcanoes. One of them was sharp, where all the others were smooth. "I've found it!" I held the orb up, and counted, working out exactly which peak matched the spiky one on the orb. "It's that one, there. Dentro, can you take me down?"

～

Identifying the correct volcano was one thing. Getting inside it was quite another.

We were low over the basin of the volcano, the heat from the bubbling lava washing over us. No part of me actually relished the thought of being back in the oppressive heat, but I needed to complete the task and show Hephaestus I was worthy of his help.

"I believe that you should drop the orb in," said Dentro.

"What? But what if I need it?"

"I agree with the dragon," said Zeeva.

I gave her a long look, trying to work out any alternative options. Coming up with none, I swallowed and gripped the rock. "Fine."

I drew back my arm, then launched the orb into molten rock below. It made a small splash as it hit, then sank slowly into the lava.

"It didn't work," I breathed as it disappeared. "What in the name of fuck am I supposed to do now? I threw away the damn orb!"

Heat swelled over me all of a sudden, then the lava began to whirl, almost as though someone had pulled a plug underneath it. In seconds, a dark black hole appeared. "I am not jumping into that," I said, staring.

But a vision of Ares filled my mind, his sensual, powerful gaze boring into mine. For him, I would jump into a volcano. For him, I would do anything.

"Allow me to help you," said Dentro, and gently lowered me toward the hole. When I was ten feet above it, I heard his voice again. "I can get no closer to the heat, fierce one. Good luck." Then his tail uncoiled from around me and I was dropping.

I suppressed a shriek and grasped at the thought of the horse shield, dragging it around myself as I tipped into darkness. But almost immediately I felt my weight taken, and a deep fiery glow bloomed around me.

I was floating gently down through another forge lining the inside of the volcano, just like Hephaestus', with platforms housing vats of lava and creatures working with hammers and tools beside them. Lava flowed from the top of the volcano all the way down, filling the vats then spilling down, until it reached a pool at the bottom.

The smell of sulfur was overwhelming and I used my power to block it as whatever was causing me to float started to pull me toward a wide platform. A huge figure was hunched over a slab, beating something that was glowing white-hot with a flat hammer. He turned as my feet met the platform, and ripples of heat washed over me from the vat. I felt my stomach flutter as I found my footing, whatever it was taking my weight vanishing and the sensation jarring. When I was certain I was steady on my feet I looked up. And up.

The man towering over me was an actual giant. And he only had one eye.

"Hello," I said, feeling *Ischyros* hum against my chest. I longed to pull the weapon from my bodice, but was pretty sure that would send the wrong message.

"My master sent you. You had an orb. Why?"

His voice was raspy and booming. Other than the one eye thing, he just looked like a normal guy, if a normal guy was a twenty foot tall wrestler, wearing only a pair of hessian shorts.

"I, erm, need to collect a couple things for him," I said. "I'm Bella, by the way."

He blinked and bent over to look closer at me. The smell of sulfur battered against my defenses. "I am the famous cyclops, General Brontes. I am sure you have heard of me." He beat a giant fist against his bare chest.

"Of course I have," I said quickly.

"Good. What do you want?"

"Some gold and a purple phoenix feather, please."

His solitary eyebrow lifted. "The gold I can give you, if you are strong enough to carry it."

"I'm strong," I assured him.

"You don't look strong." He screwed his face up and peered even more closely at me.

"Well, I am."

He shrugged. "The feather needs to be fetched from the stores."

"OK. Where are the stores?"

He pointed down. "Under there." I moved and peered over the edge of the platform.

"Under where?"

"The lava."

I blinked at the simmering pool of molten rock. "Oh. How do you get to them?"

"You don't, unless you are a telkhine."

"What's one of those?"

He shook his head, then began to lumber along the platform. "Come," he said. I hurried after him. "There. That is a telkhine." My mouth fell open as I looked where he was pointing. Over at the next vat there was a creature working that looked like nothing my wildest imagination could have invented. It was as though a seal and a dog had been combined, and then the thing had been given webbed fingers. The top half of the body was mostly dog like, but the bottom half consisted of a squat fish tail that it was propped up on. It was working on something that looked like a chainmail net, its hands moving so fast I could barely keep up with them. The sight was kind of mesmerizing. "My master created them to work in his forges. They are master smiths and they can swim in lava." Brontes said.

"Wow. OK. Will he get the feather for me?"

"Absolutely not."

I snapped my eyes to Brontes. "Why not?"

"Telkhines hate everyone."

"Oh. Could you ask him for me?"

"No."

"Please?"

"No. If you want the feather, you must go through the lava to get to the stores yourself."

I opened my mouth to argue, but Hephaestus' words came back to me. This was a test of my worth. Of course it would not be as easy as asking someone else to do it for me. "Fine. I'll go myself. Please can I have the gold first?"

"Yes, but I still do not think you are strong enough to carry it."

"We'll see about that, Mister General," I scowled.

. . .

I followed the enormous cyclops back to the slab he had been working at, and he began hunting around for something, moving lumps of metal and tools I didn't recognize around. I shifted uncomfortably in the heat, wishing I wasn't wearing a damn dress. The tight bodice wasn't so bad, and kept my sword safe, but the skirts were sticking to my thighs in the humidity.

"Here," Brontes said, and turned back to me. He was holding a small bar of gold in his hand, not much bigger than a candy bar.

"That's it?"

"Yes. That is all the mighty Hephaestus will need. Gold from his forges is like no other."

"I appreciate your help," I said, reaching out to take it from him. He dropped down into a crouch abruptly, and I almost stumbled back in surprise as a single eye came level with me. He had a mop of dark, scruffy hair, and thick lashes.

"When you die in the lava, I would like the sword you are carrying."

"What? Firstly, no. Secondly, I'm not going to die! How do you know I am carrying a sword anyway?"

"I am the general of smiths. I can feel it. It is a fine thing."

"It is a fine thing," I agreed and reached out again for the gold. "And it belongs to me. Now, please may I have the gold and I'll be on my way."

Brontes cocked his head at me, then handed over the shining metal.

"Fuck me sideways," I gasped as he placed it into my hand. It weighed a freaking ton. I almost dropped it before my power kicked in, amplifying the strength in my arms, making my skin glow in the process.

"Huh. You can carry it," muttered Brontes, then straightened with a nod. "You will probably still die in the lava."

"Well, aren't you a ray of freaking sunshine?" I scowled, trying to get the impossibly heavy little piece of metal safely stowed in my bodice. *Ischyros* was hot against my already-too-hot chest, and seemed to burn even harder as the gold slid in next to it.

Brontes frowned at me. "I hate sunshine."

"Then it's just as well that you live in a volcano. How do I get to the stores once I'm in the lava?"

"Just go straight down."

"OK. Anything else I should know?"

"I will take good care of your sword once you are dead."

"It's my sword! Keep your hands off!" I snapped, then shook my head and stamped toward the steps carved into the interior of the volcano, leading down toward the pool of lava.

"Well, shit, that's hot." Fear was making my insides clench as I stood over the pool. It bubbled and oozed, mostly a rich orange but glowing white in places. I didn't actually know if I could survive swimming in lava. I knew I was immortal, as Ares didn't have any of my power. And I knew I could use my shield.

But, as much as I was loathe to admit it, I *was* a baby

goddess. I didn't really know how to use my power properly, and I was alone.

Ares filled my mind instantly, as though my head was railing against the word *alone*. I wasn't alone anymore. I had Ares. A man who thought like me, understood me, loved me. Didn't want me to be anyone else.

I took a deep breath, and pulled my shield around myself. This was the only way to save him from the curse. If I had to swim through fucking lava for him, I would.

With a muttered curse, I jumped.

6

BELLA

I t's so hot, I'm going to die. I sucked in non-existent air as I began to sink through the heat, the sentence repeating in my mind, no other thought able to get past it. *It's so hot, I'm going to die.*

Nothing could survive this heat. I was suffocating, my eyes were burning, I was sinking. The weight of the gold was dragging me down, and my legs were kicking uselessly.

It's so hot, I'm going to die. There was nothing else but the inferno. My skin was melting off my body, my eyes were streaming so hard I could see nothing.

It's so hot, I want to die. The chant had changed. I couldn't take it. I was done. The heat was unbearable, it had to stop. I couldn't breathe, I couldn't move, I-

My feet hit something solid. The mental chant cut off, and I kicked hard instinctively. I heard a faint sucking sound, and then the ooze around me was lessening, lessening, until I was falling though air. I came to a thumping halt on hard rock, knocking what little air I had left in my lungs out of me. I heaved in breaths as I felt the rock beneath me, trying to orientate myself.

The rock was warm, but it wasn't searing.

"Oh thank fuck." I rolled onto my back, pressing myself against the floor gratefully and trying to steady my breathing. My eyes widened as I took in the view above me. It was as though the ceiling was made of glass, a barrier between the room I was in and the mass of surging lava.

"Can I help you? Are you hurt?"

I started in surprise at the timid voice, and tried to sit up. The gold in my bodice was weighing me down, making it hard to move, and I patted myself down, feeling for burns. To my surprise, I could find none.

"Erm, I'm fine," I said, turning on my ass to look for the owner of the voice.

A telkhine, much smaller than the one I'd seen with Brontes, was standing up on its tail a few feet from me. Huge racks of shelving filled the room behind it, and the light was all coming from the glowing lava above us, making everything look orange.

"We don't get many visitors down here. Who sent you?"

There was no aggression in the creature's voice, just curiosity. But Brontes had said telkhines didn't like people. I decided to err on the edge of caution.

"Hephaestus sent me. I need a purple phoenix feather. Do you know where I can find one?"

The little telkhine nodded enthusiastically, its face lighting up. "I sure do. The feathers are my favorite."

Hope surged through me as I looked at the creature.

There was no way this thing wanted to hurt me, I thought, as it's weird webbed hands clapped together.

"What's your name?" I asked, getting to my feet slowly.

"Mikro. Because I am small. I work in the stores, because I'm too small to work in the forge." There was a note of sadness to the slightly female voice.

"Well, let me tell you, I like it better down here than up there," I said with a smile.

"Really?"

"Yeah." It was a lie. It was even more claustrophobic with the lava oozing over our heads than it was before, and just as hot. As if it wasn't bad enough being inside a volcano, I was now under one.

Although even that was better than being in the lava. I shuddered and shook myself, trying to rid my body of the memory of sinking through the liquid inferno.

"You know, you're lucky. It would have taken you ages to get to the bottom if that gold wasn't weighing you down. And it's a good job you had something made by Hephaestus on you, or you'd never had got through the ceiling," Mikro said.

"Really?" I assumed she could sense *Ischyros* and the gold with the same blacksmith magic Brontes had.

"Yes. If you didn't have that sword, you would have just sunk to the bottom and stayed there."

I felt a bit sick at the thought, and patted my chest. "Thanks *Ischyros*. Once again, you've saved my ass," I whispered.

Mikro beamed at me. "You make your sword happy,

and that makes smiths happy. Come with me and we will find your feather."

We wound through the shelves, Mikro talking fast about her job in the stores as we went. I was only half listening, my body still humming with adrenaline, and filling with impatient hope. I was vaguely aware of the huge sheets of metal and alien looking tools we were passing, but one thought was dominating my mind. Once I got the feather, I could return to Hephaestus. And then I would be one step closer to Ares.

"Here we are."

Mikro had come to a stop and I looked at the shelves next to us. It was like a freaking magical mardigras. Feathers of every type I could possibly conceive, and then some more, were fanned out in a display of dancing light and color.

"I can see why they're your favorite," I breathed in awe.

"I know! They're beautiful."

"They are." My gaze was caught on a giant peacock feather that was rippling with teal light the same color Zeeva always flashed.

"That's for Hera only," Mikro said seriously, and I snapped my eyes away.

"Of course. Which ones are phoenix feathers?"

Mikro pointed to a row of feathers on one of the lower shelves and I ducked into a crouch, scanning them. They were as long as my forearm, with soft fluff at the base, tapering into magnificent smooth curves at the top. I pointed to a purple one, the exact shade of the plume on my crushed helmet. "I think that's the right one," I said.

Mikro nodded, and plucked it from the shelf. "Then here you are. Keep taking care of your weapons, and they will take care of you," she chirruped happily, before handing me the feather.

"I will, and thank you." But my words were lost, because the second my fingers closed around the feather, I was flashed.

The God of Blacksmiths stood before me, exactly as I had last seen him at the edge of the pool of lava. He was holding the crushed helmet and he had the hint of a smile on his misshapen face.

I nodded deferentially, then pulled the heavy gold from my bodice. "I have the feather and the gold."

"Good. Bring them to me." He held out his other hand, and I hurried forward to give them to him. Power rolled from him, a sense of calm stoicism that clashed against my own fierce energy.

The god turned away from me, limping toward the mass of lava, and I inched closer impatiently as he crouched down. He flared with a sudden golden light, and dipped the helmet into the liquid fire, along with the gold and the feather. I drew in a breath, concerned his hands would burn, but he straightened and lifted the helmet high.

It was glowing as golden as he was, and something stirred deep in my chest as the god's hands grew, closing around the metal. Heat, but internal - the kind of heat *Ischyros* gave out - spread through my body as Hephaestus' light got brighter and brighter. Just when I thought my skin may actually catch alight, he opened his giant hands.

They moved fast, and I saw that he was molding the now supple metal, a look of intense concentration on his fascinatingly misshapen face. Within seconds, the helmet was the right shape again, and Hephaestus' hands began to shrink back down. He reached out a long arm, the helmet held carefully in his fingers. I took it, warm tingles of power thrumming through me immediately. It felt exactly like *Ischyros*, which flared with heat against my chest from where it was safely stowed.

"Thank you." My voice sounded almost reverent. "I'll be worthy of it, I swear."

"Good. Now leave."

I didn't need telling twice. I had a beautiful, savage god to save.

"Why are you doing this?"

I knew my roared question would receive no answer. And I knew my pain would only give Aphrodite more pleasure. But I couldn't bear the torment any longer.

When I thought of Aphrodite my head cleared, the anger flooding my veins directed purely at her. I knew what she had done. I knew she had taken something from me. Something I deemed more important than anything else. But the second I focused on what that was, the anger boiled over, no longer directed at the Goddess of Love but at *everything*.

I wanted to kill everything. I wanted to fight, to maim, to prove to the world that the God of War could not be beaten or bested, that I was the strongest being alive. The red-mist would descend and then... Then I would come round, I didn't know how much later, my body broken and bleeding. I could not recall the reason through my fury-fueled haze, but I had no power. No divine strength, just that of a well-muscled human. Which I could see was no match for the forest around me.

After the first black-out I had deduced that I had let my rage loose on a tree, the torn skin and blood all over the bark, and the wounds on my hands and bare feet my evidence.

After the second I found a dead wolf at my feet, its throat torn out. Deep lacerations clearly caused by teeth covered my wrists and hands, where my armor did not reach.

The third time, I knew the bones in my right hand were broken. The pain made my head spin and my stomach churn.

The fourth, my left ankle was snapped, the bone jutting right out of my skin.

Each time the rage got the better of me, more of my body suffered. Soon, I would not be able to stand or use my hands at all. But I knew I would still try, when the blood-lust settled.

I took a rasping breath, trying to hold the image of Aphrodite in my mind, and stop the slip of my thoughts to whatever it was that she had taken from me. Whatever it was that I needed so badly, that made my heart pound and the drums beat. An image of a woman, fierce and proud and shining gold filled my mind suddenly, and I screamed as my broken hand closed into a fist, agony lancing up my arm. I was pushing myself off the forest floor before I could stop myself, red descending over my vision, coloring the bleak forest the hue of blood.

Death. Death to all, and victory to Ares. There was no other way.

"Ares!"

I spun at the voice, ready to kill, ready to win. My pain was gone, and I was ready. *Ready for war.*

"Oh god, Ares." The voice broke, and a figure burst out of the undergrowth. I stumbled, then stopped. For a moment, I thought my heart had stopped too.

Bella.

It was Bella.

She was wearing a golden helmet which meant that I could only see her eyes, but I was sure it was her. Memories of the woman standing before me tumbled through my mind, and for a second of pure bliss, I remembered. I fell in love with her all over again.

But then fire was coursing through me, a darkness filling my veins like acid.

Win! Win! She has your power, take it! Win!

The voice was deafening, and I reached out, the cord connecting us bursting to life. I pulled, hard. This was what I needed. I needed my power. Then I would be whole again. Then I would be strong again. *Zeus would respect me again.*

I needed my power back.

But none came.

"Ares, what have you done to yourself?" The woman's voice was choked, and I could see pain filling her eyes.

"Give me my power!" I bellowed, ignoring the scratching pain in my throat. I took a step toward her but my leg gave out. I was aware of the sensation in my lower half, and of the woman's cry, but it only made me more angry. "This infernal fucking body! Give me my power, now!" Desperation was coursing through me, tipping me dangerously close to fear. *Why couldn't I reach her power?*

"Ares, please. I can't see you like this. Please, let me help you."

"Never! I take help from nobody!"

She moved toward me and I lashed out. I missed. More anger swelled through me, impotent rage making my vision cloud. I was Ares, Olympian God of War. I was afraid of nothing.

"You said we would help each other. You said you loved me." The rage stuttered a second, and I tried to focus on her but my other leg gave out. "Ares, you need to know that I love you too. I feel the same. I love you."

Almost as though I'd taken a blow to the head, I fell backward. My armor hit the moldy earth, my broken body bouncing inside it, but I didn't notice. The woman's words echoed through my head as everything faded around me.

I love you.

Nobody loved me. My subjects revered me, the gods respected me, but nobody loved me.

"Why?" I heard the word leave my own lips as my vision swam in and out, shining gold moving in a blur over the top of my prostrate body.

"Because you are strong and proud and good. You're fierce and magnificent, and you're mine. Mine, Ares. And I am yours." Intense emotion filled her voice, and I knew her words were true. I knew it as surely as I knew that I was dying. "I love you."

The cord that connected us seared white-hot all of a sudden, and I heard her cry out.

"Bella!" Concern for her overpowered everything else. The red mist drained away instantly, the toxic rage filling me receding into nothingness.

"Ares! Ares, I need to heal you." Her voice was both relieved and frantic, and my vision cleared long enough for me to see her lift her helmet away from her beautiful face. Tears streaked her cheeks, and she clasped her cool hands to my burning skin.

Then her face faded into blackness.

8

BELLA

"Please, please, please heal." I felt sick to my soul as I stared down at Ares' scratched, pale face. Any skin that his armor didn't cover was ruined; torn and bloodied. One of his hands was clearly broken, the bones at nauseating angles, and his left ankle was practically split in half, blood pouring from the wound in terrifying quantity.

I knew it was a risk to remove the helmet. If the curse was still in place he could come round and drain my power. But he had already lost so much blood, it was clear that if I waited a moment longer he would die. He had no power, no immortality, and no ability to heal himself while I was wearing the helmet.

He had recognized me, before he had passed out. I had heard it in the way he had shouted my name, seen a flicker of it in his unfocused eyes.

"Please heal," I said again, hot tears tracking down my skin. "And please remember me. Believe me. I love you."

. . .

"Well, aren't you two cute?"

I whipped my head round at the sugar-sweet voice that I knew belonged to Aphrodite. My instinct was to leap up, to draw my sword and take the evil bitch's head from her neck. But I couldn't take my hands from Ares. He needed me. He couldn't draw my power from me; I had to pour it into him.

The Goddess of Love took a step toward us, a beacon of beauty and light in the miserable, faded forest.

"Fuck off, Aphrodite. If he dies, I will find you and I will end you."

She gave me a smug smile. "If the almighty Goddess of Chaos can't best me, I highly doubt a backwater baby deity like you will fare any better." Alarm trickled through me.

"You fought Eris?"

Her smile widened. "I outsmarted Eris," she whispered. Her voice was lyrical, sensual, compelling. I slammed my protective walls around my mind. I couldn't put the helmet back on; Ares needed my power.

"Where is she?"

"As if I would tell you. Let's just say it will be a long, long while before she finds her way back home."

Red tinged the edges of my vision. Eris might have been a colossal pain in the ass, but I had become inexplicably fond of her. She had helped us. And I believed that she cared more for her brother than she admitted. "What happened to you to make you so cruel?"

Aphrodite's eyes darkened.

"There is nothing more cruel than love, Bella. I am responsible for providing the most intense feeling of bliss anyone is capable of feeling. Love. There's nothing like it. But everything exists in balance." A bitter look crossed her ethereal features. "I was born with the ability to cause more pain than any other God alive."

"That doesn't mean you should!"

She straightened abruptly. "My motivations are none of your business, little girl."

"Why are you here?" Tension was making my muscles ache, and fear was building in waves that crashed through me. To fight her, I would have to let go of Ares. And that might kill him. I couldn't let go.

But I sure as fuck would not go down without a fight. Carefully, I pictured the horse shield, willing a protective dome around us that she would hopefully not see.

She chuckled. "Bella, I'm ancient. I can sense your pathetic magic."

I snarled, keeping the shield up. She wouldn't be the first to underestimate me and regret it. "What do you want?"

"To say goodbye." Her voice was quiet, and carried a lethal danger. "To Ares."

Fear tore through me, rage taking over and feeding my power like rocket-fuel. The dome around us burst into flame, and Aphrodite stumbled. "You will not take him!" I screamed.

I could only see her silhouette through the flaming dome around us, but her voice was clear. "I am as bound to my power as every other god. You genuinely love him, and I can't interfere with that. But trust me when I tell you Bella, I will not stop until you are both dead."

The flames leaped and grew, and with a roar I pushed as much power as I could spare from Ares into the dome. The boom was so loud that pain lanced through my skull. Everything around us flashed white as the flames became impossibly hot, bursting out like a nuclear explosion.

"Next time, little girl." Her voice rang in the aftermath of the boom, but before I could answer her, I felt Ares stir beneath me. Heat surged through my palms. I snapped my eyes to him, hope and relief and a million other emotions filling my chest.

"Bella." The cord that connected our power flared to life, and I felt the tug in my gut.

"Ares, take it, take my power. Heal yourself." My voice came out as a sob. He was alive. He had spoken my name.

"Bella," he said again, his eyes still closed. The pull got stronger, and I glanced away from his face to his ankle. The blood had stopped flowing.

Reflections of the inferno all around us danced across his golden armor, and I tipped my head back, trying to stop my tears.

"Aphrodite?" I yelled. But I knew she had gone. Something touched my hand, the one glued to Ares' face, and I gasped, looking back down.

Ares' palm was over my fingers, the bones straight again. His eyes were fixed on my face, and for a heart-stopping second he just stared at me. Fear that the curse had not been broken bubbled up inside me, my breath getting short. But then he spoke.

"Mine."

And I knew he wasn't talking about the magic. Intense, soul-deep adoration took over his face as he stared. He was talking about me.

I was his.

9

BELLA

"I thought I was going to lose you," I breathed, gripping his face harder.

"Never. I will never lose you, and you will never lose me." His voice was getting stronger, and the pull on my power was steady now.

"You were so... broken." A lump the size of a golf ball seemed to have lodged itself in my throat. "I couldn't bear to see you like that."

Shame washed over his features, but his eyes only dipped from mine for a fraction of a second. "I am truly sorry that you saw me like that. I... I know I tried to kill you." He looked sickened.

"No, you misunderstand me," I told him. "I meant seeing your body broken, the life leaving you. I couldn't bear to see you like *that*."

Ares' beautiful face creased up in confusion. "But what about the blood-lust? The wrathful, savage rage?"

I gave him a small smile as I shrugged my shoulders. "I knew that was within you the first day we met.

It's your ability to control it that makes me admire you so much."

The confusion leaked from his face, replaced by wonder. "You are like nobody I have ever known," he whispered to me.

"Ditto," I told him.

"All those years..." He trailed off, fear flicking through his eyes.

"What? What do you mean?" It was my turn to frown.

"Just that I wish we had found each other sooner."

My shoulders relaxed. "We have found each other now, and that's what matters."

"Aphrodite will not make our lives easy," he said, trying to sit up. Reluctantly, I released my hold on his face, helping to pull his shoulders up. He was almost a dead-weight, and the color leeched from his face again, but he persisted. His jaw dropped when he looked around himself.

We were sitting in what was essentially a crater, the rest of the forest burning and crackling gently around us.

"What happened?"

"I, erm, caused an explosion. To try to stop Aphrodite from killing you." Ares blinked at me and I shrugged again. "I think it worked." My smile slipped as her words crashed back to me. "She fought with Eris, and she says she won. She said that it will be a long time until Eris finds her way home."

Anger crossed the god's face, but it melted away as he gripped my hand in his.

"Eris is strong. We will help her if we can, but only after we finish what we have started."

"The Ares Trials," I said quietly.

"Once we are free of these abhorrent games, we can..." He didn't finish the sentence, a haunted look crossing his face instead.

"I don't love Joshua," I said in a rush, suddenly scared that he might think I would leave him if we rescued my friend.

"I know. You love me. I can feel it." Warmth filled my whole body as he gazed at me. "But we must finish the Trials."

I nodded. "Yes. I can't leave Joshua a soulless victim of a rogue demon - he's my friend. And we need to get you that Trident."

"Bella, I... I need to tell you many things."

I nodded again. "I know. I saw your mother."

He stiffened. "What? What did she tell you?"

"That we were bound, but not by her. That I have lost memories, and that prophecy won't permit her to tell me more. That she loves you." Ares closed his eyes. A tree cracked nearby as it lost its battle with the flames, causing a loud thud as the wood hit the earth.

"Bella, I need you to trust me. I need you to wait until the Trials are finished before I tell you what you want to know."

"Why?"

He opened his eyes, looking intensely into mine. "Because if we fail the Trials, one of us will surely die. Only one of us can be immortal."

"What has that got to do with you telling me about

my past?" Apprehension skittered through me, my stomach knotting.

"Please, Bella. Trust me." It sounded like the words pained him, and I was sure I could see guilt in his tight expression.

But, I *did* trust him. I couldn't help it. "You're making me nervous," I told him. "Is it really bad? Whatever it is that you won't tell me?"

It was definitely guilt on his face. "It is... not good. It will take some time to understand. Time and focus that we can't spare until the Trials are over, and the demon is returned and your friend is safe."

I considered his words. He wasn't lying or sugar-coating anything, which strengthened my trust in him, despite it worsening my feeling of dread. He was being practical, true to his nature.

For the first time since arriving in Olympus, I thought about what it would be like *not* to find out where I came from, or how I'd ended up living so many miserable years away from Ares and Olympus. If it was as bad as it sounded, perhaps I'd rather not know.

Either way, Ares was right about one thing. Making sure Joshua was safe and regaining his power and immortality was more urgent. I knew how important mindset and focus were in a fight. His words rang through my mind. *"If we fail the Trials, one of us will surely die."* I'd survived this long without knowing whatever it was he didn't want to tell me. The knowledge wasn't worth risking our lives, or Joshua's, for now.

"OK. We fuck the Lords over by smashing the shit out of these Trials, and then you tell me everything."

A smile pulled slowly at Ares' lips as he let out a sigh of relief. "You know, you swear too much."

"So I've been told."

A shadow moved behind Ares and I almost jumped to my feet before recognizing Dentro's form.

"I have to be honest, fierce one, I was quite looking forward to destroying this accursed forest myself," the dragon said.

"Sorry, Dentro. It was kind of an accident."

"You have done a thorough job."

I grinned at him. "Thanks."

"I wanted to warn you though, Panic is not pleased. And nor are many of the previous inhabitants of the forest. I would advise leaving Skotadi with some haste."

I looked at Ares. "Are you strong enough to flash us?"

"Yes. I think so."

"Thank you for everything, Dentro," I said, standing up and reaching out my hand. Slowly, the dragon slid across the charred ground, his massive body seeming to repel the burning embers. He stopped when he reached me, lowering his head until it bumped against my palm. A sense of peaceful contentment washed through my whole body.

"It is I who needs to thank you. Call me if you ever need me."

Flashing us drained the strength from Ares completely, and I was so caught up in breaking his fall as he crashed to his knees that I didn't even register where we were.

"Ares!"

"I'm fine," he slurred, then his eyes rolled, and he fell unconscious again, sliding down my body, his huge weight almost taking me with him.

"Shit," I cursed, trying to lower him to the floor gently. He had color in his cheeks and his wounds were healed, so I knew it was just exhaustion that had taken him this time, but a small flutter of panic rippled through me regardless.

I noticed the floor as I carefully laid his head down; a rich, shining wood. Running in planks... I looked up sharply, examining my surroundings. I was on the deck of a ship, shining solar sails standing out against a soft, cloudy sky. I yanked *Ischyros* from my bodice, the blade shimmering and morphing immediately.

Had something gone wrong with Ares' flashing? Had someone else flashed us back to the demon's ship?

But as I turned warily on the spot, I realized that I was definitely *not* on the demon's ship. This vessel had only one raised quarterdeck, and was much smaller, and the front formed a sharp triangular peak, almost like a Viking ship. The deck was made from a richer, darker wood, and the finishes over the doorway that I could see ten feet away were gleaming gold. As I looked closer, I saw images of weapons carved into one of the two masts. The ship gave off an air of arrogant opulence, somehow.

"So this is the God of War's secret home?"

Zeeva's voice didn't startle me, a sure sign that I was becoming used to her appearing out of nowhere.

"Secret home?"

"All gods have their public palaces, and the places they actually like to spend their time. The latter are generally kept a secret." Movement caught my eye, and I looked over to see her sauntering toward the railings. I walked to her, peering down over the side of the ship.

"That's freaking awesome," I breathed.

Below us, under the clouds, was an island that looked like a patchwork of little worlds. A jungle city spread across the south-east cliffs, and I could see sand-filled deserts nestled between expanses of moorland and snowcapped mountain ranges. A colorless forest with a blackened center caught my eye. "Skotadi," I realized. "This is Ares' realm."

"Yes."

"It's stunning."

"It's lethal," answered the cat, wryly.

I suddenly felt as though I should be sharing this moment with Ares, and turned away, moving back to him. The world below us wasn't going anywhere, and I wanted to wait for a guided tour from the god himself. "I need to get him comfortable. He needs to rest."

Summoning my magical strength, I managed to get Ares through the door and down a small flight of steps.

"Fuck, your armor is heavy," I told the sleeping god. I stepped into a wood paneled corridor with massive double doors at the very end. They were grand enough that I was sure there would be a nice room behind them, so I headed that way.

I was right. The room was beyond nice. It was freaking epic.

Columns of mahogany shelving lined the walls like ribs, and between each one was glass, from floor to ceiling. Glittering clouds floated by on either side of us. A plush red rug dominated the room, flanked by two huge black leather couches. I carried Ares to one, and set him down carefully, before spinning to look more closely at the room. Another set of massive double doors faced the ones I had come through, and on either side of them were cabinets filled with weapons. A glowing spear, a bow strung with something gleaming gold, a war-hammer with etchings that moved even as I looked.

The shelves intersecting the glass sides of the ship were covered in books, weird little artefacts, and many different bottles.

"Zeeva, which of these is nectar?" I knew how much the stuff had helped me when I had been drained.

"Behind you. Third shelf."

It was Ares' voice that had answered me, and I spun to him, heart leaping. "You're awake!"

"I am."

"Good. Where the fuck are we?"

He was sitting up, looking groggy. "This is where I live."

"You said you liked ships; you didn't say that you lived on one!" I moved to the shelf he had indicated, finding the nectar and an array of glasses on the one below.

"This ship doesn't sail very far. I have the best view in Olympus here."

"I saw. Will you tell me what all the different kingdoms are?" I couldn't keep the excitement from my voice as I turned back to him, two filled glasses in my hands.

"Of course I will." He smiled at me. "Your enthusiasm is alien to me."

I scowled as I sat down beside him, passing him his drink. "Is that good or bad?"

"It is good. So very, very good. I had forgotten what joy and excitement had felt like. Until you."

I felt my cheeks heat, and happiness made my stomach flip. The man had no filter for his thoughts at all, and it appeared that included the gooey ones. "Well, thank god for that, because not everyone appreciates my enthusiasm. I have been called annoyingly hyperactive in the past."

"Anyone who insulted you is an asshole."

I barked a laugh. "Hey! That's my word. You're not allowed to use it."

"I've come to quite like it."

"I've come to quite like you," I said playfully, then instantly felt stupid. Ares was the God of War, a giant of a man, a freaking legend. How did one flirt with a god?

"Just *like*? Maybe there's something I can do to increase my appeal a notch or two." Hunger gleamed in his now clear eyes, and I gulped. It looked like normal flirting worked just fine with this god.

Ares drained his glass of nectar, the wicked gleam still in his eyes. "Come," he said, and stood up, proffering his hand to me. I took it, expecting him to lead me through the closed double doors, but instead he headed through the doors we had come through. I turned my head, catching Zeeva's eye.

"I'll leave you two alone," she said, a lilt of amusement to her voice.

We emerged on the deck a couple of minutes later, and Ares paused, inhaling deeply. Then he pulled me to the railing, looking between the island below him and me.

"My realm, my woman," he said, his face set and strong. A drum beat in the distance. *My woman.* I was his woman.

"You're feeling better then?" I said, my voice coming out a little breathless. A flame fired to life in his eyes.

"With your power running through my body, I feel invincible. With you, I feel like I can do anything."

More flames danced to life in his eyes, and the drum beat again. He reached to his side, and with a few movements his armor fell with a clatter to the planks. His shirt beneath was torn and bloody, and his pants loose at his waist. I looked back to his tangled hair and fierce eyes. He looked like he had been dragged through hell and back. *And survived.* It was the hottest thing I'd ever seen.

Heat flooded my core, an ache building instantly, all the fire and passion and intensity from the castle rushing back like a tidal wave. He took a step toward me, towering over me.

"You have turned my world upside-down. You have made me question everything I thought I knew. You have made me new enemies. And you have given me a reason to *live.*"

The drums beat harder, and louder, my heart hammering in time with them. My pulse raced as I stared up into his flaming eyes; his power, his strength, his sheer presence utterly dominating me. I was his. Completely and eternally. I had never needed anything more than I needed him.

"You are everything," he rasped, voice choked with desire, then he was there, his arms around me and his lips crushed against mine. He kissed me with almost frenzied intensity, and I matched him, my need as strong as his. His hands were in my hair, pulling my face to his, but mine immediately went to his chest, pushing their way between us. I was desperate to feel his hot skin against mine, to believe that this was really happening.

He stepped back, breathless, and pulled his shirt over his head as I raked my nails down his rock-hard abs. I bit down on my lip as he hooked his thumbs into the waist of his pants, and pushed.

"Holy fuck." I actually said the words out loud, though I didn't mean to. The glitter-filled skies of Olympus and the liquid gold solar sails of the ship paled into non-existence in the presence of Ares' nakedness. He was perfect. Thick and long and so, so hard.

He growled deep in his throat, then pulled me to him, his fingers trying to work at the corseted dress. I couldn't stop my own fingers reaching for him and I gasped as he tensed. I couldn't close my hand around him.

"Leave the dress," I panted, letting go and pulling the skirts up around my waist. I wasn't waiting a freaking moment longer.

Ares grasped me around the waist with his huge arm, then spun me with his other, pressing my front into the railings, and his chest into my back. With his other hand he reached around, grasping my jaw and pulling my head back. For a second I thought my knees would buckle as his hot mouth met my neck, his teeth nipping at my skin as he worked his way down to my shoulder. I pulled at my skirts, wriggling my panties down and moaning as I felt him press against my bare cheeks.

"Bella," he growled, moving himself between my

legs and pressing me harder against the railings. His hand pulled my jaw further round so that he could kiss me.

"I need you," I murmured into his lips. He pressed into my wetness, just a little.

"I love you," he breathed back, then his mouth took mine as he pushed hard into me.

Pleasure like none I had felt before rocked through me, and I cried out even as he kissed me. The arm that was wrapped around my waist tightened and lowered, holding me close as he moved, pressing against the rest of my exposed sex. He kissed me everywhere he could reach as I gasped over and over, firing tingles from my neck and shoulders right through my body, as though they were wired to my core. Wave after wave of new sensation and pleasure pulsed through my body, and I gripped the railings so tight my knuckles were white, as something incredible built inside me.

He moved harder and faster, keeping time with the drums, and I lost myself utterly to the rhythm. Then he moved his hand over me faster, slowing his pounding thrusts, and suddenly every single inch he moved felt exquisite, and I was exploding around him, a noise I didn't even recognize erupting from my throat. My legs did buckle then, and the railing cracked loudly.

Before my alarm could detract from throbs of intense pleasure running from my head to my toes, Ares scooped me up. I protested at the sudden lack of him inside me, but within seconds he had me pressed against the main mast, guiding his huge self back to where he belonged.

"You're fucking beautiful," he breathed, kissing me, resuming his thrusts with even more power than before. The receding aftershock of my orgasm fired back to life, and I found myself in a state of bliss I couldn't even register properly, somewhere between releases, every stroke of his tongue, his fingers, his cock, divine.

When I felt him stiffen, then let out a roar of pleasure, my second release came instantly, and I wrapped my legs tightly around him, burying my face in his neck. I was exhausted, in the most incredible way. A way that was completely new to me.

"So good," I mumbled into his skin as he pressed me to the mast, our skin slick with sweat.

"So good," he agreed, his voice hoarse.

"You swore," I said, pulling my head up and looking at him. His skin was glowing gold, I realized, and I could see an expression in his eyes that I thought might be contentment.

"It was worth it. You are fucking beautiful."

I kissed him softly, my lips hot and swollen. "I love you," I whispered when we parted. A solitary drum sounded in the distance as Ares looked deep into my eyes.

"I will always love you."

11

BELLA

"So what's that one?" I pointed to a tundra-like wasteland at the north-west point of Aries, far below us as I leaned over the railings.

Ares tightened his grip around my waist before he answered, pulling my back against his bare chest. "That's Pagos. And see that mountain range just a bit further along? That's Terror's kingdom."

Unease tightened my chest, and I pressed myself closer to Ares' warmth as I stared down at the jagged, snow-covered mountains. I had been very deliberately avoiding thinking about the last Trial, not wanting the bubble of bliss I was experiencing on Ares' ship to end.

"I guess it won't be long until they announce it," I mumbled.

"I imagine not, no."

"Terror is the worst of the Lords, isn't he." It wasn't a question.

"He is the strongest, and hardest to control."

"What do you think he'll make us do?"

I felt Ares shrug behind me. "Something terrifying. But we're stronger than them, Bella. We were strong before, when we were at odds with each other." He gripped my shoulders, gently turning me to face him. "Just think how strong we can be together."

"Like when we fought the Hydra," I whispered.

"Yes."

"Ares, only one of us can be immortal at any point. And... I don't know how you feel but..." I trailed off as I stared into his determined face.

I wasn't sure how to say what I was thinking. Or even if I should say what I was thinking.

All fighters had a weakness or two. It wasn't possible to have none. But the good ones had very few. *Almost* nothing to lose. There had to be something at stake, or nobody would fight at all, but for the winners that would often be pride or ego.

The truth was, I had never fought with so much at stake. With so much to lose.

Ares could die. And deep down, I already knew that I wouldn't let that happen. When pushed to the point of making a decision between losing him, and living my own life, I knew what I would do.

Which was bat-shit fucking crazy. Everybody I knew who had fallen in love in the past had fallen out of it again. I'd barely known the guy a week, and I still had serious reservations about some of his personality traits.

Our relationship could surely not have reached die-for-each-other levels this fast?

I would set the world alight to keep him alive.

The thought speared through the doubt and confusion, hot and permanent. And I was ninety-nine percent certain he would do the same for me. There was zero point in denying it, the knowledge that his life was bound to mine felt like it was branded on my soul.

"I dislike seeing you so serious," Ares whispered, and leaned forward to kiss me. His touch was like a tonic for my spiraling concerns and they scattered back to the shadows of my mind.

One thing at a time, Bella, I told myself as I fell into his embrace.

We got three more hours together to enjoy the ship and each other's company, before the urgent presence of Terror pressed against our minds.

Cold anger wound its way through me at the intrusion. The longer I spent lounging with Ares on his bed or on the couch, talking, laughing and kissing, the more I wanted that life to be normal. I wanted the Trials over, his power back, Joshua safe, and the secrets of my past dealt with. So that we could get on with being together. So that I could show him everything he had been missing in his own world.

"You have not made things easy for yourselves," Terror's voice hissed through my skull as I lay against Ares, dozing in and out of a lazy sleep.

"Where and when is the Trial?" barked Ares, moving to sit up and dislodging my head from where it had been nestled on his chest.

"My mighty Lord, I am pleased to hear you sounding so well." His tone dripped with sarcasm.

"Where and when?" Ares repeated.

"The final ceremony will be in my throne room in two hours."

His presence vanished and I scowled and flopped backward onto the pillows. "Do the gods in Olympus not mind that everything is done with fuck all notice?"

"They have to make an eternal life exciting somehow," he shrugged.

"By having spontaneous parties? I can think of better ideas."

"And I can't wait to hear them."

"Really?" I rolled to my side to look at him. His playful smile dipped.

"Bella, I have thought hard about mortality. And glory. And what our power stands for. I think that we can try some new ideas in Aries."

Hope made my smile widen, and I sat up on one elbow. "I have so many freaking ideas. And I want to see everywhere, and meet everyone."

Ares chuckled, then moved quickly, pushing me onto my back again and covering my body with his. My skin fired with heat, all my muscles clenching. "Just remember, it's my realm. Not yours. Got it?" He dropped his head, nipping at my neck. A small moan escaped me as he pressed his hips against mine and I felt how hard he was.

"I'm sorry, I couldn't hear you," I told him, and he raised his head from where he was planting kisses across my collarbone.

"I said, it's my realm, not yours."

"Nope. All I'm hearing is Bella, do whatever you like in my realm."

Fire flashed in his eyes. "I do believe that you are trying to wind me up." I had time to see the predatory hunger flash in his eyes before his mouth met mine and all other thoughts fled.

~

"Dare I ask why you have women's clothing here?" I heard the dangerous tone in my own voice as I stood in front of the open closet in Ares' bedroom.

"Eris. She hides here sometimes, when she has angered the wrong person." Trepidation rumbled through me at the mention of the Goddess of Chaos.

"Is it our fault that something has happened to her? If she hadn't been helping us then Aphrodite might have left her alone."

Ares stood up, the toga he had donned falling to his knees. His expression was hard. "Bella, let me assure you that the feud between those two runs far deeper than you can imagine. And Eris is one of the strongest beings in Olympus. If Aphrodite bested her, she did it with help. You must not blame yourself."

I let out a sigh. "The first thing we do, after all this is over, is find out what happened."

Nervousness flitted across his face, and I didn't think it was to do with Eris. "The first thing we do is talk. About you. And then we can try to find my sister."

"Right," I nodded. An innate reluctance rose in me.

There was no doubt that telling me about my past was a conversation Ares didn't want to have, which meant, by proxy, that I didn't want to have it much either. Anything that threatened the bliss we were creating for ourselves was unwanted.

But it couldn't be avoided. Eventually, I would need to know, and it seemed to be weighing heavily on him. What could be so bad?

What if he's done something you can't forgive?

That was my true fear, I realized as the question settled. That was the real reason I no longer burned with curiosity about who I was. Because my feelings for Ares now burned hotter.

"Will her clothes fit you? I can show you how to change them with magic if not, but it won't be as good as what Eris can do." I forced my attention back to the closet.

"That's sweet of you, thanks."

Ares screwed his face up. "Sweet? You may be the first woman in the world to describe me as such."

"And I'll be the last. If I hear any other woman call my warrior god sweet, I'll punch them in the nose." I narrowed my eyes at him and he grinned. Seeing a playful smile on his serious face was still new enough to me that it made my heart flutter, and heat swirl through me.

"You know, I might like to see that. Perhaps I will start trying to get girls to call me sweet."

"Don't even think about it, armor-boy."

12

ARES

Having Bella on my arm when we arrived in Terror's throne room felt more right than I could understand. I needed the world to see her with me. I needed everyone to know that she belonged to me.

She had selected one of Eris' more formal dresses, and to my surprise she had chosen to keep it the way it was. I was both pleased that I could see so much heavenly cleavage, and furious that others could too. I had a suspicion that that was exactly why she'd worn it. The corseted top half was a deep grey, like iron, but the color changed slowly in what she had told me with a chuckle was called ombre, into creamy ivory at the bottom. The whole thing was covered in a lace decorated with gold feathers, and together we had used her magic to change them into plumed helmets. "After all, we both have helmets now," she'd grinned at me.

We spelled the helmet itself to transform into a headband, like mine, though hers was more delicate and had a deep purple gemstone in its center. Against her ash blonde hair it looked sensational. *She* looked sensational.

I would kill to see her smile. Hell, I would do any damn thing she told me to, without question. Not that I'd tell her that.

What would she do when I told her the truth about her past? About what I had done?

A part of me that I wasn't even sure had existed until I met her, held some hope that the connection between us would be strong enough for her to forgive me. But the larger part of me feared that I would lose the one thing I had ever cared about.

I thought I'd cared before, about war, glory, honor. Aphrodite. But everything paled next to the fierce Bella, her power and strength and courage burning brighter than anything in Olympus.

She was true love. She was my purpose. She was everything.

"You're sure he's not going to make us go straight to the last Trial from the ball? I am not doing anything in this dress," she hissed next to me. We were waiting in a line of guests to walk through a shimmering portal at the end of a corridor. I knew this was the only way to reach Terror's ballroom, as I had been a guest before, but I didn't want to tell Bella what to expect. I wanted to see the surprise on her face when she saw it. Terror was the most mysterious, dangerous and egotistical of the Lords, and both his kingdom and his palace matched his personality.

"You have your sword and helmet if he does. That is the most important thing."

She nodded. The guests in front of us were turning frequently to look at us, muttering and smiling excitedly. We were the guests of honor.

Bella was fidgeting by the time we reached the portal, energy thrumming from her.

"Are you ready?" I asked, tightening my arm around her smaller one.

"I've been ready for fucking ages," she answered impatiently, and stepped through the portal, tugging me with her.

Her mouth made an O shape and then she blew out a long breath as she took in our new surroundings. We were standing on a long platform jutting out from the side of a snow-capped mountain. Twinkling blue lights danced overhead, not bright, but strong enough to add to the dusky light coming from the sky above us. Short columns acted as tables and guests gathered around them with their drinks and canapés. A dark archway set in the mountain had a steady stream of servers moving through it with trays. Snow, powder soft, fell but never settled on the floor, and an artificial warmth encompassed the whole platform.

Bella moved toward the edge immediately, staring out at the looming mountains. There were jagged blades of rock jutting from the snowy peaks and spearing the sky, and pitch black crevices everywhere that could be hiding any manner of danger. They almost seemed alive with menacing energy.

"The mountains are impressive," I said.

"Foreboding as fuck," she answered, still staring.

"Do you fear them?"

She glanced at me. "They call to me," she said quietly. "Danger and mystery and the thrill of the unknown."

"I am flattered, but you should be careful what you wish for." Terror's voice was as unpleasant as it always was, and my muscles tightened in reaction. We both turned to him, and I was surprised to see that he was alone. Ink-black shapes crawled unsettlingly across his marble frame. There was no better body for the spirit of Terror and, although I was sure I had chosen well, I took no pleasure in his company.

"Where are the other two?" asked Bella.

"Around," he said dismissively. "Did you wear a dress covered in helmets to anger Panic? I like that." His tone dripped with malice. "You should have added some dragons too. He's most upset about the loss of his pet."

The bond connecting me to Bella was so much stronger now that I felt her surge of anger. "That creature is no pet," she snarled.

"Not any longer, no. Are you ready for my Trial?"

Fear trickled through me and I knew at once that it was his influence. Here, in his palace and without my full power, I could not stop his magic. Bella pulled her arm out of mine and the fear intensified alarmingly before she twined her fingers with my own. Heat rushed me, forcing out the tendrils of building terror. But she was gripping my hand hard enough that I knew it was affecting her too.

"We are ready," I said, glaring at him. "And when we have won, we expect the demon to be handed over without delay."

"You know, we never discussed what would happen if you lost." I opened my mouth to reply, then realized with a sickening jolt that he was right.

"If we lose, we likely die," I ground out.

"An immortal Olympian?" There was a delight in his tone, and it was clear that he knew that I was no longer immortal, unless I took every ounce of Bella's power. "No, no, mighty one. We need a bigger risk than that for you. If you lose, then instead of us giving you the demon, we get you."

"No. Absolutely not." Bella's grip turned vice-like and her voice was as sharp as a blade. Her reaction was just what Terror wanted. Fear, anger, challenge. I would make sure that he got nothing he wanted.

Before Bella could say any more, I began to laugh. A small chuckle at first, that turned into a mocking boom. Terror stiffened, his featureless face fixed on mine.

"What do you plan to do with me?" I asked, plastering my best maniacal smile on my face. I drew power slowly from Bella.

"Whatever we wish," hissed Terror, the cockiness

gone from his voice. He definitely hadn't got the reaction he had hoped for from me.

"OK, little Lord. If we lose, you get me." I stepped forward, growing a foot suddenly, and dropping my voice menacingly low. "But when we win, I assure you that I will be shattering this pretty body of yours into a million tiny pieces, and finding a new host for Terror."

To the Lord's credit, he didn't step back, though his stone body did twitch. I kept my eyes locked on his featureless face, focusing on the power of War. Screams sounded in the distance, and the cries of battle and the stampede of hooves were joined by the booming of explosions. The smell of fire and blood washed over us, and heat rose around me.

The challenge hung in the air, Terror's black swirls the only thing moving.

"May the best man win," the Lord said eventually.

"We will."

Terror turned, stalking back to the other guests, and no doubt the other two Lords.

"You know, you're sexy as hell when you do that."

I looked at Bella, happy to see a flush to her cheeks that suggested she really did find me attractive. "I'm glad you think so." Power was circulating through my body, the encounter firing me up, leaving me longing for a fight.

"What if we lose?" Bella asked quietly, her flirtatious tone replaced with just a hint of doubt.

"We won't. We can't." There was already enough at

stake in these stupid games. I wouldn't accept that there was any chance of us losing, so there was no harm adding one more thing to the list.

"Why do they want you?"

"Dominance. If they rule the God of War, they rule the realm. The desire for power is in their nature. It's what they were created to do."

"But you control your nature, why can't they?"

I took a breath, her words making me uneasy. So fast had we fallen for one another, yet there was still so much she didn't know about me. About my power, and what I was made of. About what I had done to keep my sanity.

"Bella, they are the reason I *am* able to control myself. When Pain, Panic and Terror were a part of me I was... different. Bad. The only way to control them was to split them up and put them into exceptionally strong-willed hosts, with their own kingdoms to keep them occupied. When they are combined in one being they are too strong. They are the very essence of the worst parts of War." I shrugged. "But they are still forces to be reckoned with, and they always work together. This is not the first time they have tried to rise against me and it won't be the last. The difference is that I have never been without my power before."

"Well, you have your power now. You have me."

A blue glow from the fairy-lights danced in her eyes, and after a second's hesitation I pulled the helmet from my head, using her power to turn it into the headband.

"You're stunning," I told her, my chest fluttering as she took in my face.

"A perfect match for you then," she grinned, as I leaned down to kiss her.

We strode around the ball like we owned the place, exuding a confidence I knew would anger the Lords. Whether Bella truly carried that confidence, I wasn't sure, but she seemed happy to act as cocky as I was. Panic gave us a grimace-like smile when we neared him, but did not speak with us. And, as I had expected, Aphrodite was nowhere to be seen.

The mountains really did seem to call to Bella. She seemed to be zoning out of polite conversation with the endless stream of curious guests who wanted to meet the girl who had coaxed the miserable God of War out of his helmet, staring at the looming summits instead.

I felt the same. I could sense the danger within them and it was like a magnet, pulling me to prove myself. I needed to fight, to win, to revel in victory. And I knew with the same certainty Bella seemed to have that the sharp, ragged mountains held a mighty challenge.

By the time Terror drew everyone's attention to him, I actually wanted him to confirm that the last Trial would involve this stark and lethal kingdom.

"Thank you all for joining me," his icy voice rasped. "The last test in the Ares Trials is a simple one. Climb one of my mountains. If you reach the top, you win. If you do not reach the top, you lose."

Excitement surged through my veins. It was exactly as I had hoped. I felt a bolt of energy from Bella, her skin glowing briefly gold.

It was time to show everyone how strong we were together.

13

BELLA

My excitement to tackle the mountain fizzled out slightly when the light from the flash faded and the reality of our task set in.

"Wow. That's quite a long way."

It was freezing cold, and although I was wearing a shirt with sleeves under my leather armor, and my helmet over my head, the cold air still bit at my skin.

We were at the base of a mountain formed from shining black rock, and covered in snow. Everything was jagged, not a smooth line in sight, as though a giant had taken a hammer to the whole surface, leaving jutting angular spikes and deep crevices everywhere. There was the hint of a path before us, twisting up into the mass of rock. And when I tipped my head right back, I could only just see the white peak of the mountain.

"Climbing will be hard, and I expect there will be

some added challenges on the way," Ares said, armor-clad and humming with pent-up energy.

"It looks like Terror. All black and white," I mused as Ares started forward toward the path.

"You're right. It does."

"I like hearing that." I followed him, my boots crunching on the snow. *Ischyros* was warm in my right hand. "Feel free to tell me I'm right as much as you like."

Ares threw a glance over his shoulder at me, his eyes sparkling. "You'll have to earn it."

I shrugged. "Not hard. I'm always right."

The God of War snorted. "I highly doubt that."

We bickered playfully for an hour or more, before it began to snow. The path wasn't really a path, just a groove that meandered between the sharp boulders. The incline was steep, and I wasn't sure how well I'd be doing if I didn't have my power. The magic-less version of me was fit for sure, but we weren't climbing an ordinary mountain. There were no trees or scrubby bushes at all, just craggy black cliffs and rivulets of ice. There were no sounds of animals or birds, or anything living, even when I used my new super-senses to hunt for signs of life. All I could get from the mountain was an ominous magnetism. It was creepy and compelling all at once.

My power kept me from getting numb from the cold, but it didn't stop the snow being annoying. The visibility dropped quickly, forcing us to slow our pace a little.

"How long do you think it'll take to get to the top?" I asked.

"Two days. But I believe there will be obstacles to overcome. So perhaps longer."

I nodded, even though he was in front of me and couldn't see me. There was no way Terror's mountain didn't have more in store for us than just snow.

"What was that?" We had been trudging up the ever steeper mountain-side for longer than I cared to know, and I had just seen movement that wasn't snowfall for the very first time.

"Where?" I felt the slight tug of Ares drawing my power and I knew he would be enhancing his senses just as I was. We were entering a reasonably level clearing, surrounded by dark boulders, and I pointed as we slowed.

"By that rock," I whispered. I could just make out the sound of soft footfall, and the slow, steady breathing of something that wasn't Ares. The climb had yet to be steep enough that we had needed two hands, so we had both been walking with our swords drawn. I felt a burst of excitable heat from *Ischyros*, tingling down my arm and causing adrenaline to flood my system.

There was a flash of white, and something green moved again behind the rough boulders.

"Show yourself!" Ares shouted the command, and my heart hammered in my chest as we stood side-by-side.

A rumbling snarl echoed through the clearing, then everything fell silent again.

"What is it?" I hissed.

"I don't know yet," Ares answered, through gritted teeth. We were both beginning to glow.

Out of nowhere, a huge blurred mass of white and brown and green barreled into Ares, knocking him to the ground just a foot from me. I invoked the power of War, snapping the image of myself on the stallion into place instinctively. As everything around me slowed and turned red, Ares leaped back to his feet, sending the creature that had attacked him skidding backward.

It was like nothing I had seen before, even at the ceremonies the Lords had thrown. Most of it looked like a snow leopard, with beautiful spotted markings, huge green eyes and small tucked in ears. But the rest of it...

"It has two fucking heads!" The exclamation was out of my mouth before I could stop it. There was a second neck protruding from the snow leopard's body, and it ended in a vicious-looking mountain goat's head. Coarse black horns curled angrily from its skull and its eyes were beady and red. The leopard head pulled its lips back in a snarl, baring its teeth at the same time that the goat head hissed, clacking its jaws together.

"Three. Check the tail," Ares said. He was right. The end of the snow leopard's fat bushy tail was a freaking snake head, bright green and as dangerous-looking as hell. "It's a chimera."

The creature pawed at the snow-covered ground before us, and I tried to suppress my admiration and astonishment at seeing such a beast.

"How do we stop it?" I didn't want to kill it. "Will fire scare it off, like the oxys?"

"The cold on this mountain will douse magical fire quickly."

The chimera growled, loud and menacing.

Before I could offer another idea it pounced again, this time at me. I was ready though.

I threw myself to the side a second before it hit me, swiping at its legs with my sword as it landed on the ground instead of on me. The snake tail whipped around, forcing me to bring my sword up to defend myself as a forked tongue darted out.

Ares' golden glow appeared behind the chimera, and before it could turn to where I was crouched he brought his sword down. There was a ringing clash as the goat head moved to meet him, its horns blocking his blow.

I rolled, keen to get out of the snake's reach, and as I straightened I found myself face-to-face with the leopard head.

"Fuck, you move fast," I cursed as I jumped backward, only narrowly avoiding the snapping jaws. The goat neck was longer though, and pain slammed through my shoulder as it butted hard into me. I stumbled backwards, then the thing shrieked, an ugly animal noise that made my insides feel weird. Ares had hold of the chimera's tail and was yanking it hard away from me, the snake's head snapping and straining to reach him. The creature turned, its legs moving fast to try to get out of the god's grip, but Ares was too strong. The chimera stilled as Ares brought his blade down, stopping just an inch from the tail he was gripping.

"You can't beat both of us. Come after us, and you will lose one of your heads," Ares said loudly. All three mouths hissed in response.

Ares let go, and I held my breath, sword ready.

The snake head reared back now that it was free, but just as it looked like it was going to launch at Ares, the leopard head made a screeching sound and it froze. With one last hiss, the chimera turned in a slow circle between us, then bounded away, lost in the shadows of the boulders in an instant.

I relaxed my sword arm a fraction, and sent some healing magic to my bruised shoulder. "Is it me, or was that too easy?" I asked slowly.

"Chimeras are usually solitary creatures. But if she returns with a pack, we will be facing a tougher adversary."

I stared after the incredible animal, and hoped like hell that she didn't have any friends on the mountain.

We resumed our trek, and were forced to sheath our swords when the incline steepened and the ground became less stable. Soon we were climbing properly, using both hands to pull ourselves up crumbling slopes, The physical activity would have felt good if the mountain wasn't sending such increasingly bad vibes at us.

"Why didn't you cut off the snake head?" I asked Ares, when we stopped for a short breather.

He looked at me from behind his helmet. "Put it down to my new appreciation of mortality." I raised my eyebrows at him. "And I knew you would rather I didn't. It's the chimera's home we're invading after all."

"If we weren't wearing helmets, I would kiss you," I told him. I knew mercy was a part of war, and I also knew that Ares did not kill indiscriminately. But the red mist was a powerful thing, and instincts often prevailed in a fight for most people, let alone those with divine strength. My admiration for his self-control was only growing.

"If we were wearing nothing, there is no part of you I wouldn't kiss," he said, and heat flared through me, chasing away the cold.

"Let's get this over with, so that you can prove that to me."

14

BELLA

The ground we were covering showed no sign of leveling out, and it wasn't long before we were practically scaling a cliff. The almost vertical slope was icy cold, and if a person didn't have magic to keep their skin from freezing or some seriously epic gloves, they would not have been able to use their hands at all.

I was surprised by how much concentration was required to keep me moving up the rock, and the constant draw on my power to keep myself from freezing to death was starting to worry me too. Only one of us could be immortal, and a fall to the jagged peaks below would surely be fatal. If we both fell...

The thought caused a very unwelcome fear to hover over me, and I began to pray for flatter ground. Or even more chimeras.

Every time the rock crumbled under my grip or my boots slipped on an icy patch my heart lurched and a little more of my composure fled. Not knowing where the top was made it even worse.

"You're doing great." Ares' deep voice filtered through my mind, providing a massive wave of comfort to flood through me. I had paused, clinging to the rock for a moment to gather myself while I had a fairly decent ledge for my feet. He must have noticed. I glanced down, seeing him ten feet or so below me, and tried to ignore the dizziness that accompanied looking in that direction.

"So are you," I told him.

"I am used to climbing; I sense that you are not?"

"It's not something I did back in the mortal world, no," I admitted. *"I'm becoming tired, having to concentrate so hard."* I didn't voice my worry about only one of us being able to survive a fall. And now that I had looked down I was pretty sure that even if I did survive a fall, it would take a colossal effort to try again. That's if I didn't freeze to death whilst healing.

There was no question that this mountain was dangerous for immortals, I realized. That was probably connected to its twisted lure. Danger personified.

"Don't let the fear get to you. Use your confidence. This is Terror's trial, he thrives on fear. So will the mountain."

I tried to wrap Ares' words around me like a blanket, taking comfort from them. *The mountain makes you more scared,* I told myself. *You don't get scared. So climb the damn mountain.*

.   .   .

When the ground finally started to level out, I didn't let myself believe it at first. I had found a rhythm that I didn't dare risk disturbing, one that buried the growing fear of falling under the simple practice of putting one hand and foot in front of the other.

But as the snow fell softly on us, I couldn't ignore the fact the ground was starting to catch it, and that my body was starting to tip forward more with each step.

When it was flat enough that I could stand upright I turned, waiting for Ares.

"Are you alright?" he asked as he reached me, eyes full of concern.

"Yes. Relieved."

"In that case, something worse is likely coming. We can rest soon, my love."

I nodded, pleasure filling my chest at the endearment. I had never been called "my love" by anyone before. With renewed determination, I hauled my tired ass up the rocky mountain path.

"Trees!" It probably wasn't normal to get so excited about the piss-poor excuses for trees that had somehow managed to grow on the bleak mountainside, but I was sick to death of looking at snow. They were scrubby and spindly and barely had any leaves, but they were definitely trees.

Ares gave a small snort. "Barely," he said.

"Well, they're better than rocks."

"Hmmm."

The ground was a lot less steep now, but the path

was twisty and narrow. We were likely wasting time following the path instead of trying to find a more direct way up, but the rocks clawing their way out of the ground on either side were spiky and awkward, and some were three times my height. It would be too hard to try to navigate them. So we continued to stamp along the path, and I continued to admire the crap trees interspersed between the crap rocks.

"I don't like this mountain as much as I thought I would," I said into the silence.

"Stay alert," was Ares' only response.

I blew out a sigh, then frowned as I felt answering warm breath on my shoulder. I turned my head quickly, but there was nothing there. Slowing my pace, I blew out hard again. A warm gust blew over my back and I whirled.

There was nothing.

"What's wrong?"

"I can feel warm air."

I could make out Ares' scowl behind his helmet. "That seems unlikely. I can't sense anything here."

I pushed my own senses out. He was right. No animal sounds or smells nearby. Frowning, I began walking again.

The next time I felt the gust, I could swear it was accompanied by a shove. Not a hard one, but I was sure I felt something make contact with my shoulder. I slashed with *Ischyros* as I spun, but my blade met thin air.

"There's something here, Ares."

As if in response to my words, the snow flurried

suddenly, making me unable to see more than about ten feet in any direction. Something shoved into me again, harder this time, and I yelled out. Ares' armor clanged and I looked over in time to see him stumble.

"What the..." Before he could finish the sentence the snow stopped as suddenly as it had started, leaving us both looking stupidly around in circles.

"Do your show yourself thing," I hissed.

Ares cast me a look, then shouted. "Show yourself!"

Nothing.

We waited a moment more, then Ares shrugged. "We're wasting time. Let's keep moving."

I didn't argue, but I kept *Ischyros* clutched in both hands and my body stayed tense as I followed him. I didn't like foes I couldn't see one little bit.

15

BELLA

Nothing had happened for another hour or so, when my skin began to crawl, unpleasant tingles snaking down my spine. Something was watching us, I was certain. But when I sent my senses out I could find nothing.

The feeling of being watched increased minute by minute. The number of trees was increasing too, and the new ones were actually able to hold some foliage. I scanned the leaves warily, trying to feel for signs of life coming from anything that might be hiding in them. The path had narrowed even further and started to wrap around the body of the mountain. There was now a steep slope to our right heading down, and an even steeper slope on our left, heading up. We had checked to see if we could scale it but it was covered in a sheen of solid smooth ice, impossible to grip.

The wind had picked up, causing the sparse leaves to rustle and cold flurries of snow to gust over us. One such gust whipped across the path, and for a moment I was sure I heard a voice, as though it were carried on the wind. A child's voice.

You're tired, I told myself. *There are no voices on this mountain.*

But another breeze blew over us, and this time the voices were clear. High-pitched childlike voices, repeating the same three words.

Blood. Die. Eat.

Goosebumps rose on my skin and my chest tightened. "Ares? Do you hear that?" I could hear the uneasiness in my own voice.

Ares didn't answer, he just keep walking ahead of me. "Ares?" I called louder. Another gust hit me, harder, and the childish voices were loud whispers, rippling with excitement.

Blood. Die. Eat.

Blood. Die. Eat.

"Ares!" There was fear in my voice this time when I called out, and my legs began to move fast, jogging to catch up with him.

I grabbed at his arm when I reached him and he jerked in surprise. "Bella! Something is here." His eyes were wild and unfocused.

"I'm hearing a bunch of kids who want to eat me on the wind," I said, my voice breathless. "It's creepy as fuck. What are you hearing?"

"The same," he said, and I knew he was lying. But now was not the time to try to find out what exactly creeped out the God of War.

"What is it?"

"I don't know, but there's nothing living here, or we'd feel it."

"So... It's dead?" My voice caught on the word dead.

"I don't know. I suppose it must be. Or something powerful enough to hide its presence."

I hoped fervently for the latter. Somehow, the idea of a powerful magical creature was easier for me to stomach than the idea of ghosts or zombies.

The snow started to flurry again, and a juvenile laugh rippled through the air. There was a screech, an awful sound that made me feel sick, and I felt fear bolt through me. I gripped Ares harder, looking uselessly around myself.

Blood. Die. Eat.

Something shoved my back, and Ares went down with me, both of us landing hard in the snow. More laughter sang around us, and as I scrambled to my feet I realized that the red mist wasn't coming.

"I can't fight what I can't see," I blurted, hating my rising panic.

"Use your shield," Ares said. He moved to me, gripping my waist. "We'll do it together."

"Yes. Shield," I repeated, staring into his eyes and trying to swallow my fear.

The next time we were shoved, it bounced off an invisible dome around us.

Blood-

Before the child's voice could say the next word I poured power into my shield, and the words cut off.

Immediately the terror that was building inside me, spreading though my body, lessened.

"Good." Ares still had a slightly unhinged glaze over his eyes.

"Ares, I'm too tired to keep the shield up and walk. But there's no fucking way I'm sleeping here, with whatever's out there. What are we going to do?"

"We have to get rid of it," he said after a moment's thought.

"How? It's freaking invisible."

"We think it's connected to the wind?"

I nodded in agreement, rubbing at my arms. I could feel pressure against the shield, an awful scratching sensation against my power. I hated it. "Yeah."

"Then let's make our own wind. Blow it away."

"Really?"

"I can't think of anything else to try."

Making wind was as simple as making fire, Ares explained to me. I just had to think about it, and throw my power behind it.

"We'll do it together on the count of three. Drop the shield, then blast this whole cursed path with wind."

"What if it blows us off the path?"

"It won't. But get low, in case whatever it is blows back."

I nodded, dropping into a crouch. The ground was cold, the snow piled inches high.

"Three, two, one!"

When the shield dropped the voices were shrill and taunting, a hideous screeching sound whistling through the air.

Blood! Die! Eat!

I poured everything I had left into what I pictured as a tornado, and with a roar the swirling column of wind burst into existence. Red tinged the edges of my vision, and hope lit up inside me, forcing out some of the tension and fear.

"Go," I willed the tornado, and it began to move along the path. The voices warped, the words no longer clear, and the tornado was louder than the screeching as it roared along the path. I willed it to grow and move, clearing away whatever it was that was trying to haunt us. It pinballed around on the narrow path in a zigzag, whipping up the spindly branches on the trees and causing a torrent of snow to splatter in its wake.

It avoided the place Ares and I were crouched though, and by the time it started to die down my power was completely spent.

"Did it work? Are they gone?"

Ares didn't reply, his face set in concentration. I tried to do the same, but fatigue was setting in. I didn't feel like I was being watched though, and the creepy as hell voices were silent.

"I think so."

"Thank fuck for that. I need to sleep."

We heaved a few boulders together, and pulled a few leafier branches from the trees around us to build a makeshift shelter. I was keen to get as much rest as we could whilst the cannibal kids were gone. They could come back at any time, and the thought frightened me. Invisible scary spirits were seriously not my thing. Ares assured me that my power would keep me warm enough while I was unconscious and, trusting him completely, I was out the second my head hit my trusty backpack.

When I awoke, Ares had one arm wrapped tight around me, pressing me against his golden armor, which even in the mountain weather was always warm. I was alert the second the sleep cleared from my mind, wary of what might have woken me. Sparsely-leaved branches were propped across the top of the two boulders we were between, and I took it as a good sign that they hadn't blown away.

"Ares," I said, lifting his arm and sitting up. I reached instinctively for my helmet, sitting proudly next to his. Energy tingled into my gut from the cord connecting us as he stirred.

"Kiss me," he murmured, and I dropped my head, planting a soft kiss on his mouth.

"We've got to get going," I said, pulling back. His eyes were bright, the sleepiness leaving him fast.

"I am bored of this mountain now," he said as I crawled out of our shelter and pulled my helmet on. It was featherlight once it was on my head, as though it became a part of me. It obscured none of my vision and I never felt it move.

"Me too." I scanned the snowy path. It looked identical to how it had before we slept. I felt inside myself for my power, finding the ball of energy under my ribs full and hot. Ares emerged from between the boulders and yanked on his helmet.

"Let's try to get to the top today," he said.

"Definitely."

16

ARES

"One of the realms must be your favorite," Bella pushed, as we kicked our way through deepening snow. The path was still winding its way up the mountainside, occasionally turning steep and rocky, and sometimes icy and flat.

"Only my own," I answered from behind her.

"You can't choose your own, that's cheating. Pick one." She clambered over a particularly sharp outcrop of rock.

"My father's realm is most spectacular. His citizens live in glass mansions in the electrical clouds surrounding Mount Olympus. His palace is at the top of the mountain."

"Less mountain talk," she grumbled. "And besides, you dad sounds like a prick. Pick another one."

I sighed and she threw me a grin over her shoulder. "Fine. I like Poseidon's underwater realm. It is made up of many golden domes under the surface of the ocean. And he has lots of extremely dangerous water creatures living there." Excitement tinged my words at the thought of Poseidon's ocean monsters.

"What's your least favorite realm?"

"I do not like Taurus. That's Dionysus' realm; he is the god of wine and madness. His citizens live in large tree-houses that are impressive, and there are also many dangerous wild creatures, but you can trust nothing. Whole buildings can turn on their head with no notice, and everything is spiked with hallucinogens. I find it unsettling."

"I want to visit," Bella pronounced immediately.

"Of course you do. Is it me, or is the snow getting thicker?" I was sure that the snow was falling faster, and settling heavier around us.

"Yeah, maybe."

Within another hour the snow was falling hard, and we were having to kick our way through a layer that completely covered our boots. Visibility was poor and our pace was forced to slow considerably.

"When should we start to worry about the snow?" Bella called back to me.

"I don't know." Admitting that I didn't know things was new to me, and I wasn't sure I liked it. If it were anyone other than Bella asking, I would have ignored the question, or made an answer up. But the truth was, this whole mountain was as wild and unpredictable as she was, and I didn't have a clue if the snow was a threat or not.

"As long as those creep-ass cannibal kids don't come back," I heard her say.

Whatever the ghostly voices had been, they had upset her. They hadn't done much for my calm control either.

A deep, distant rumble caught my ears, and Bella paused in front of me. "You hear that?"

"Yes."

She glowed briefly as she stretched the limit of her senses. "It's coming from deep within the mountain," she said, turning to face me. There was a slight spark of fear in her eyes. "The rock itself. It's not a creature. We can't fight a mountain."

"Stay calm." I caught up to her and reached out, touching her warm skin. The rumble came again, louder, stronger. I felt it through my boots.

"Ares, we are surrounded by tons of rock and snow." Panic edged Bella's voice. *"Tons."*

"And we have magical shields," I told her, projecting confidence through our connection.

"What if we're separated?" She practically whispered the words, and I realized that was what was causing her fear. Something separating us on the mountain.

"We won't be." I gripped her hand, and the rumble gained more volume. "And even if we are, we are bound. We will find each other." I looked into her eyes, and flames flickered to life as she stared back at me. Flames of will and determination, driven by the strength of her love for me. I knew what she was feeling because I was feeling exactly the same, and our emotions flowed through our bond like a raging river.

She nodded. "OK." The ground lurched under our feet, and we stumbled. "And if we fall down the mountain?"

"Then we start again." *If we fell off the mountain, one of us would die.* I didn't add the statement that ran through my head, though I was sure she knew it as well as I did.

"Fuck starting again," she said, her face fierce as the rumbling grew and the rock beneath us shook. "We need to get away from the edge."

We moved through the snow as fast as was possible, tucking ourselves close to the mountain as we powered on. The tremors continued, but they weren't strong enough to take us off our feet.

We walked for another hour or more, the terrain becoming invisible through the pelting snow, and we were unable to relax for even a second with the frequent lurches of the ground. Rocks crumbled and rolled past us, and great slabs of snow regularly tumbled from ledges above us, forcing us to throw up our shields.

"Something's here." Bella had to shout the words back to me, the growling of the ground and the cracking and crumbling of rock was so loud. I pushed out my senses, finding a mass of something ahead of us. Something powerful.

Fighting whilst trying to stay steady on this cursed mountainside would not be easy. Excitement and adrenaline fired through me, forcing out the doubt. Bella and I could defeat anything. "Good! I am bored of this trek," I shouted back.

"You know what? Me too." Her words were strained and I knew she was forcing as much confidence into them as possible.

"We will not be separated, my love." I sent the words to her mentally, and a wave of warmth flooded my gut, flowing from our bond.

Before she could reply though, the whole mountain shuddered and a brilliant flash of teal light seemed to erupt through the snow. Freezing powder flew everywhere, sharp lumps of ice accompanying it, and we snapped our shields up. Bella moved, throwing herself as far away from the edge as she could as the ground shook even more violently. There was a slow, echoing crack and I threw myself after her as a tidal wave of snow began to crash toward us.

"Bella?"

"I'm here. What happened?" I rolled, the surface beneath me feeling like warm glass and everything in complete darkness.

"I got the shield up in time... but we're submerged."

A faint light filled the space as Ares began to glow. I sat up, getting my bearings as I looked around myself.

He was right. We were in a bubble completely surrounded by snow. "Erm, how much air do we have?" I tried to keep the rising fear from my voice and failed.

"Plenty, don't worry."

"How much is plenty?"

"Enough for many hours. And besides, it won't take us long to dig ourselves out." He moved to my side. "Are you hurt?" I shook my head. The ton of snow that had crashed down over us had made me cold, but had not been painful.

"Just a bit cold," I told him.

"We're safe in here, for now. Why don't we rest a moment? Warm up."

I raised my eyebrows at him. "Whilst buried in snow?"

"Why not? No weird voices, no chimera."

"What happens if the shield fails?"

"It will be fine, as long as we don't need to use any other magic."

I cocked my head at him, unsure how comfortable I was with the idea of being buried alive. "How much snow do you think is above us?"

"Not so much that you couldn't fireball your way out of here in a hurry if you needed to." His eyes creased at the corners, and I knew he was smiling behind the helmet. I instantly felt myself relax at the sight. His eyes were so beautiful.

"OK. I guess we could do with a rest."

"It would be good if we could find a way to warm up without using magic," Ares said mildly, pulling off his helmet.

"Huh. Got anything in mind?"

He moved, shifting so that he was sitting with his arms across his knees, facing me. All the serious tension had gone from his face and his eyes had darkened with delicious promise. "Oh yes. I can picture what I'm thinking of very clearly indeed."

I looked at him incredulously. "Are you suggesting what I think you are?"

He shrugged, a wicked smile settling over his beautiful face. "I don't know. What do you think I'm suggesting?"

"Something that we absolutely can not have broadcast to the rest of Olympus," I hissed.

"The shield is keeping them out."

"Really?"

"Yes. Check for yourself."

I sent out my senses, probing. The shield was solid, that was for sure, but I had no idea what I was looking for. I pulled my own helmet off, and ran my fingers over my hair, pushing back what had come loose from my braid.

The truth was, nothing would make me feel better than to be intimate with him. What better way to force out the fear and trepidation, the anxious energy, than to remind ourselves what we were fighting for? To take strength from one another. There was a tiny voice in the back of my mind that I couldn't quiet, adding its own argument. *This mountain is lethal. There is a very, very real chance we might not survive. This could be your last opportunity.*

"I'll tell you what will warm us up without magic," I said, making my mind up and shrugging out of my backpack.

"Please do."

"This." I yanked the heavy bottle that I had carted all the way from London across most of the most dangerous realm in Olympus, and grinned at him. "Tequila."

It was Ares turn to raise his eyebrows this time. "It warms you? Like nectar?"

"Er, sort of. It's more of a burning than warming, really," I said, unscrewing the top and inhaling the sharp, familiar scent. The amber liquid glowed in the golden light coming from Ares.

"I will drink it with you on one condition."

"Oh yeah?"

"That you are naked."

I stared at him, heat already building inside me with no help needed from the tequila. "I assume you're going to be naked too?"

"Oh yes. Naked and making sure you stay warm."

"Well, I think that sounds fair. You first." I crossed my legs, wedging the tequila bottle in the crook of my knee, and folded my arms. "Get that armor off, warrior boy."

There wasn't enough room for him to stand up in our snow cocoon, but that didn't stop him. He was down to his shirt and pants in seconds. I watched hungrily as he picked up the bottom hem of his shirt, then pulled.

Holy hell, he had a body to freaking die for. My muscles twitched as I stopped myself reaching for him, and I schooled my face into a mild expression.

"My pants don't come off until yours do," he said.

I narrowed my eyes at him, then picked up the bottle and took a swig, before handing it to him.

The liquid burned its way down my throat, and I was pleased that having godly powers didn't dull the sensation. Tequila was still excellent, even as a goddess. Keeping my eyes fixed on Ares, I began to unlace my leather armor.

"This shield better be keeping out the rest of the world," I said once I removed it.

"It is."

"Good." I pulled my own shirt up and over my head.

Ares' eyes widened, then darkened as they dipped to my chest. Slowly, his gaze came back to mine, and he took a swig from the bottle.

He swallowed, then let out a long breath before smiling. "I like tequila." With a swift movement he leaned forward, pulling me onto his lap. I squealed as he tightened his grip around me, and raised the bottle with his other hand.

"More?" Desire danced in his eyes.

I tried to snatch the tequila from him, and he lifted his arm high so I couldn't reach it. I saw my skin glow as I stretched up for it, and he spoke. "Be careful, Bella. No magic, or the shield might fail."

"I don't need magic," I said, and wriggled out of his grip.

"Oh no?"

"Nope."

I stood up over him, barely an inch between me and the top of the bubble. I had a foot on either side of his knees and he wet his lips as he looked up at me, then moved the bottle low to his side, where I couldn't get it.

"You'll have to come back down here for it now."

"Oh, no I don't. I have a better plan." Slowly, I hooked my thumbs into the waistband of my pants.

Flames burst to life in his eyes, and a drum began to beat in the distance. My heart rate sped up instantly, matching the pace.

I pulled, wriggling my ass deliberately as my panties dropped with my pants. They both snagged on my boots, but I didn't have time to do anything about it. Ares' face was inches from me, and he took a ragged breath as he took in the sight.

"You win. Here's the tequila." He held up the bottle. I took it with a grin, then yelped as his now empty hand grabbed my ass and pulled me forward. His lips pressed against the top of my thigh, and I gasped, clutching the bottle. His mouth moved fast, across the sensitive skin between my legs, then heading lower. I instinctively parted my legs, allowing him in.

His other hand came up, steadying me as he closed his lips around my most sensitive part.

"Oh god." I almost stumbled, bringing my hand down and pushing it into his hair, pulling him harder onto me. His tongue moved expertly, like it had its own kind of magic, and I felt my knees weaken as pleasure rocketed through my whole body. I felt his fingers moving up the inside of my thigh, and then he was stroking and teasing me in time with his tongue, each movement sending aching pulses of need through me. "Oh god," I breathed again as his finger finally dipped into my wetness. "I need you. Ares, I need you."

He pulled back and looked up at me, and my breath caught at the fierce hunger on his face. "You have me," he half-growled. He let go of me and eased out of his pants, revealing himself hard and ready. Desire pounded through me at the sight of him. The drums beat louder.

"Wait," he said, as I started to move. He reached down, and began to untie my left boot. "I need you to be able to move your legs." He looked at me, wicked and beautiful, and torturous longing burned through my blood. I took a deep breath as he lifted my foot from my loosened boot, then moved to the other one. Remembering the bottle in my hand, I took another swig. More fire burned through me, and suddenly, I didn't care about my boot.

Before he could stop me, I sank into his lap, wrapping my left leg around his waist and winding one arm around his neck. "I need you, Ares. Now." I kissed along his jaw as he pulled me to him, his chest heaving. His hard length pressed against me, and I squeezed my leg, lifting myself up.

He let out a long groan that matched mine as I eased myself down. The feeling of him inside me, filling me, was beyond anything I had words for. It was more than a feeling - it was a euphoria. A rightness that took me all the way to my soul. And fuck, it felt good.

I felt myself tighten as I sank fully onto him, and he froze a second. Then his strong arm was lifting me achingly slowly back up his length. Our lips met, and I sank down again, relishing him, losing myself to the waves of pleasure.

We rocked together, and I took every drop of enjoyment from each movement, letting my mind abandon every other thought I had. The small movements; the brush of his fingers across my nipples, the flicking of his tongue over my neck and lips, the soft moans he gave as I moved my fingers over his divine body, combined with the ecstasy of our bodies connecting was causing a pressure to build that I knew I couldn't contain for long. He began to move faster inside me and I ground against him, the feeling of fullness making me gasp for breath.

"Tell me you love me," he growled as he gripped the back of my neck, driving hard into me and pressing his other hand flat to my stomach. "Tell me you're mine."

I arched back as the pressure reached a crescendo, and he growled again as I gasped the words. "I love you."

They were barely audible to me through my orgasm, waves of release smashing through me, making my toes curl and my head spin. But he heard them. The connection between us flared searing hot as he came, pulling me so tight to his body that we could have been one person.

"I'm yours," I said, kissing his face and squeezing my legs around him. "I'm yours. Always."

18

BELLA

The mountain was eerily quiet when we emerged from our snow cocoon. The whole mountain side had turned white, a layer of thick snow obscuring everything. I couldn't even see the edge of the path I knew we were on. The snow was no longer falling, and barely a thing moved.

"We'll have to walk tight to the mountain, to avoid the edge," Ares said. I nodded, and we set off.

As we walked, carefully, I couldn't help the nagging feeling I'd had since the avalanche from growing in my mind. I'd recognized that flash. The color... I was sure it was the exact color Zeeva flashed with. Zeeva was Hera's minion, and Hera had teal everywhere. Was one of Hera's monsters here? Or her magic? But why? She had wanted me to succeed.

Just as I was dismissing the entire train of thought, my cat's presence pushed at my mind, through the helmet. I let her in at once, my surprise evident in my mental voice.

"Zeeva?"

"Bella, I am sorry," was all she said, and then she was gone. I stopped walking, confusion and apprehension washing through me.

"Ares, something is going on. Zeeva just spoke to me. She said she was sorry." He gave me a grave look. "Do you think something has happened? Off the mountain, I mean?" Fear for Joshua's safety bolted through my chest.

"No." Ares' voice was a rasp.

"What then?"

"I think Terror is a cruel being indeed. I think... I think he is truly going to make us feel fear. I hope I am wrong."

"Wrong about what?" Uneasiness was gathering in the pit of my stomach at his intensity. "Is Zeeva here?"

"I think so, yes. And I think Terror knows that one way to make someone as courageous as you feel true fear is to force you to fight an enemy you do not wish to. One you fear hurting."

I gaped at him. "You think he's going to make me fight Zeeva?"

"Maybe."

"No." I shook my head. "I can't. Terror couldn't force her to do anything she doesn't want to do anyway, she's too powerful."

No sooner had I said the words than there was a bright flash of teal, and a creature appeared on the path ahead of us.

My heart pounded in my chest as I took in the sight. A cat, for sure. But not the one who had lived in my shitty apartment for eight years, nor the large, intimidating cat Zeeva had turned into when I pissed her off.

This was... majestic.

She was fifteen feet tall at least, taking up almost all of the mountain path. Her tail was wrapped around her as she sat, her fur shining with light reflected from the snow. Lethal claws tipped her front paws, and where her eyes should have been were two gleaming turquoise gems. Power rolled from her, a sleek sense of danger that immediately garnered my respect. I had no doubt at all who I was looking at.

"Zeeva," I whispered, my heart hammering in my chest.

"You may not pass," she said, her voice loud on the silent mountain, but her mouth not moving.

"Zeeva, why are you here?"

"You may not pass."

"How are they making you do this?"

The gemstone eyes flickered with light for the briefest second and her voice sounded in my head. *"For this Trial, Terror is allowed to test your fear, and he is allowed to use whatever would scare you most. I have no choice."*

"You may not pass, without defeating the sphinx," she said aloud.

"I won't fight you!" The red mist was tingeing my vision, but not in readiness to fight. It was in reaction to my fury. Who the hell did Terror think he was, taking the only friend I had and making me face her? That did not instill fear in me, but anger, hot and fierce.

"You may not pass without defeating the sphinx. And the sphinx's strength is deadly."

As if to prove her point she moved fast, her claws swiping out and snagging something from the huge snowdrifts beside her.

Ares and I both had our swords ready, but then I saw what she was holding in her giant paw. It looked a lot like raccoon, but bigger and mostly white. With her gemstone eyes fixed on me, Zeeva tossed the squealing creature in the air and flicked her claw. The thing was disemboweled before it hit the ground, spattering the bright white snow with crimson.

"You may not pass without defeating the sphinx."

"No!" Panic was starting to war with the fury that was boiling through my blood. We had to get past her. We had to finish the Trial. But I couldn't fight something as strong as her and win without hurting her. "Terror, you're a fucking prick!" I bellowed the words, *Ischyros* burning in my hands. "Ares, what do we do?"

"You may not pass without defeating the sphinx," Zeeva said again.

"I know! Stop saying that!" I could feel my temper taking over, my control slipping.

"Bella, I think she's saying it for a reason." Ares' voice was inside my head, and he wasn't looking at me. *"She's emphasizing the word defeat. I think she's trying to tell you something."* I looked between him and my enormous, vicious cat. "You may not pass without defeating the sphinx." I replayed her words. She was saying *defeat*, not *kill*.

"Sphinx," I breathed, the realization hitting me. "She's a sphinx."

"Tell me a riddle," I blurted out. "If we get it right, you must let us pass."

There was a spark in her gemstone eyes before she spoke. "Three riddles, and you may pass. If you get them wrong, you will die."

"Fine." I looked to Ares. "Please tell me you're good at puzzles," I hissed.

"No."

"Shit."

"Are you?"

"Not really."

"Are you ready?" Zeeva's voice cut through my rising panic. Without waiting for me to answer, she continued. "I am the beginning of everything, the end of everywhere. I'm the beginning of eternity, the end of time and space. What am I?"

Oh god. "We should have fought her," I muttered, fear trickling down my spine. "Maybe we could have disabled her without doing any lasting damage, maybe-"

"Bella, stop talking, please. Concentrate." Ares' voice was hard and authoritative, and I closed my mouth. "Many riddles are word puzzles," he said calmly. "Let's try that first."

I nodded and tried to remember what Zeeva had just said.

"E," said Ares, suddenly.

"Correct," the cat answered.

"Wait, what?" I blinked at Ares.

"The answer is the letter E."

"Oh thank fuck for that," I breathed, letting out a huge breath. "You *are* good at puzzles. It's not like you to be modest."

"Bella, you need to calm down."

He was right. My head was spinning, the red washing in and out of my vision. "She's *my* cat. My only friend here. My only link to my past. I wasn't expecting this."

"I know, that's why Terror sent her. We can do this, OK?"

"OK. OK." I turned to the bungalow-sized sphinx that used to sleep on my damn bed. "What's the next one?"

"The first two letters signify a male. The first three letters signify a female. The first four letters signify a great. What is the word?"

I repeated the riddle in my mind, not allowing my attention to deviate at all.

"It's another word one," Ares said. "What is *a great*?"

The answer came to me in a rush. "A hero! He, her, hero!"

"Correct."

Another hit of relief smacked into me. One more to go.

"What is so fragile that saying its name breaks it?"

"Is this a word one?" I looked at Ares, alarmed to see worry in his eyes.

"It doesn't sound like it."

We both fell silent as we thought about the riddle. I repeated the sentence over and over again in my head, trying to work out what the answer might be but dismissing every suggestion that came to mind.

The silence stretched on, and I could feel the calm I'd briefly managed to get a grip on starting to slip away.

"Any ideas?"

"Shhh. I'm thinking."

I bristled at being shushed, the tension and worry in my body making me twitch. "Well, maybe we should think out loud. Standing here in silence isn't fucking helping so far," I snapped at him. He glared at me and started to speak but I held up my hand to stop him. "Wait. I think I know the answer."

Excitement thrummed though me, but I wasn't sure enough to risk shouting it out and getting it wrong. Ares' gaze intensified. "Really?"

"Silence. I think the answer is silence." He said nothing for a beat, then his eyes lit up as he smiled behind the helmet.

"I think you're right."

"Shall we risk it?"

"Yes."

We both turned to Zeeva. "Silence," I said loudly. There was a pause that seemed to last a freaking lifetime, before the huge cat answered.

"Correct. You may pass."

Without another word there was a flash of teal, and she was gone.

19

BELLA

"Honestly, if you don't smash Terror to bits, I sure as fuck will." I was stamping up the mountain path, anger rolling through me as adrenaline pumped through my veins.

"How about we do it together?"

"Ha. That would be a fucked up activity for a date." I kicked at the foot-deep snow as I powered on, the fatigue from climbing for so many hours gone, replaced with rage-fueled strength.

"It would be satisfying though. And I believe necessary. Terror is in need of a new, perhaps less clever host."

"What else is he going to throw at us on this stupid, cold-ass mountain?" I was in the mood to fight now. Fury at being pitted against my own cat had riled me up, and solving the damn riddles, although I was supremely relieved we had, had done nothing to relieve the violent urges.

A little frisson of unease at the thought of the awful

kids' voices on the wind pushed through my anger. I wanted a real fight, not creepy ghost people to fight. Which likely meant that was exactly what we were going to get next. Terror wasn't going to give us something we could defeat easily. "Where's that snow-leopard chimera with its friends?"

"I thought you didn't want to kill it? You sound ready to kill something." Ares had a mix of amusement and respect in his voice.

"Shit, you're right. I don't really want to kill stuff. Just Terror."

"Bella?"

I whirled at the woman's voice calling my name, my skin turning icy cold, and my heart almost stopping in my chest. "Bella, come here!" My gut twisted, and bile rose in my throat as I spun, looking for the owner of that sickly sweet voice.

"What's wrong?" Ares was at my side in an instant.

"My-my-" I didn't finish the stuttered sentence.

"Bella!" Fear bolted through my whole body, *Ischyros* burning white hot in response. Memories crashed through me. Awful memories. Memories I had spent a long time trying to forget.

"My prison guard," I whispered, clutching my sword with both hands.

"I'm here, Bella," Ares said, gripping my arms. "It's not real. It's just the mountain."

But as I looked into his eyes, drawing his words around me, he jerked backwards, his hands torn from my shoulders. "Ares!" I screamed as he flew backward along the snow. He roared in anger, waving his arms but an invisible force pinned him against the steep mountainside.

"Bella!" he yelled, reaching for me but clearly unable to move. I started toward him at a run but slammed into an invisible barrier. I swung my blade at it, and it went straight through. Terror's voice slithered into existence, almost as though the mountain itself were speaking.

"This test is just for Bella. Ares may not help. You must face your fears alone."

"Oh, Bella," said the female voice behind me. I swallowed, barely able to breathe as I turned.

The prison guard was standing ten feet from me, her unwashed hair piled high in a bun on her head, and a cruel gleam in her eyes. "Bella, such a fucking bad name for you." I looked at the woman as she spoke. "You're uglier than you ever were. Ugly and thick and fucking worthless. Why are you even here, Bella?"

"Leave me alone." The words barely escaped my throat. All of a sudden I was back in my cell, dark walls flying up around me, trapping me. She stepped toward me, a knife in her hand. "He doesn't love you, you broken little tramp. He's using you."

I couldn't defend myself. She'd hit me when I first went into isolation. When there was nobody there to see her do it. When I'd hit her back, she'd reported me and my isolation was extended, along with my sentence.

"Time for another haircut, Bella." She reached for my hair, jerking my head back as she caught a fist full of it. I could smell whiskey on her. "You can hit me back, but then you'll just be in here, alone with me, for even longer." Her voice was a gleeful whisper as she bent close to me.

Heat burned behind my eyes as I willed the red mist to come.

But it never had when she had made my life hell in prison. It had come at all the wrong times. It had come when I was around those who didn't deserve it. When I'd needed it against this monster, it had never come. My fear of her suffocated my strength and courage. She beat it out of me, and I could only vent it when I was out of her power, in all the wrong places.

I thought escaping her cruel tongue and starvation bribes when I got out of isolation and back with the other girls would be the end of my fear. But she still found ways to torment me, knowing I wouldn't risk being alone with her again. When I finished my time and escaped her, I vowed never to let fear win again. I vowed never to vent my violent nature in the wrong place. I vowed never to let myself stay in a place where I could be turned into a monster.

Because I knew that she would push me too far one day. She knew it on some level too, I was sure. Her goading, her abuse, was all to push me to my limit. And then it would be too late. I would have spent the whole of my life in prison for doing something unforgivable, instead of just being caught in the illegal fighting rings. She would have released the monster inside me.

Ares controlled the monster inside him. I'd seen it, in all its savagery, and he could control it. The thought spread through me, slowly at first, but buoying me as it gained momentum, my paralyzing fear and shock giving way to rational thought.

As her hot breath hit my cheek, and I felt the knife slide through my hair, I realized my fear was not of her at all. It was of losing control.

"You're not real." I croaked the words, and she paused. Slowly, she moved her face even closer to mine, and drew the knife to my throat.

"I'll feel real when this knife sinks in," she cackled.

"I beat you. I kept control and I got out. You're not real and I already fucking won." Saying the words was like a light going on somewhere horribly dark and buried inside me.

I had always considered my fear of her as a failure. But all this time, I had been the victor. I had kept control.

I moved my sword without thinking, the fear keeping me frozen in place gone. Ischyros pressed against her gut and her eyes widened as her jaw dropped. The knife fell from her hand.

"You're not real, so I could kill you if I wanted to," I said. She stepped backward, fast.

With an eerie screech, she began to morph in front of me, her sallow skin turning to pale smoke. Within a few seconds, she was gone, blown away with the snow.

"Wait!" After all these years harboring such a deep fear of the woman, I wanted more time to revel in my victory, in the realization that I had moved on and made myself a better person, despite what she had done to me. Plus, I'd kind of liked threatening her. She fucking deserved it, even if she was a creation of Terror's.

But she was gone, and the mountain path was empty, save for the snow. I turned to Ares, and Terror's voice rang out again.

"Time for the mighty God of War to take his turn." Terror's voice held barely contained glee, and it made me shiver. My body began to move of its own accord, sending me skidding hard into the mountainside as Ares went shooting to where I had been standing. His eyes found mine as we passed each other, and the fear in them made my heart stutter in my chest.

He was terrified.

He knew what was coming.

20

BELLA

"I'm sorry." His voice sounded in my head, loaded with pain. Before I could respond, a tiny wizened old lady hobbled into view.

"Why do you seek the oracle?" Her voice was deep and crystal clear, nothing like I had expected her to sound.

"No," croaked Ares. "Please."

"You wish to know if you may rule the world?"

"No! I don't want the world!"

It was as though she was hearing a different answer than he was giving.

"Such a young god, such large aspirations," the oracle mused. "You are barely born and you seek answers to questions I can't give you."

I swallowed hard as I realized what I was seeing. Ares was reliving a memory, just as I had.

"I don't need your help," Ares croaked. The oracle laughed.

"Very well. As you have traveled so far, I shall tell

you something. You are strong, but you could be stronger. There is one other who shares your strength."

My breath caught and my stomach lurched. Ares turned away from the oracle, to stare at me.

"I'm sorry," he said, barely audible.

The oracle continued to speak. "As long as she lives, you will never be immortal. A god's strength must be his own, and while it is split between two beings, you will be weaker than your brethren. If she lives, you will be stunted."

The oracle shimmered and disappeared, and a large bed snapped into existence over the snow. A young woman was sleeping in it, short blonde hair fanned out over the pillow.

It was me.

"No!" Ares shouted, as a version of him with no armor and much shorter hair strode through the snow. "Leave her!"

I barely took a breath as I watched younger Ares reach the bed and pull a shining dagger from his belt. He cocked his head as he raised it over me, then paused. Slowly, his eyes widened, softening for a split second before turning steely. He put the dagger back in its sheath, and held both his hands over my sleeping form, closing his eyes in concentration. My form began to glow a gleaming red, then vanished.

"I should have told you. I-I-" Ares cut off as the image before us changed again.

It was me, dressed in peasant clothing, bent over and digging with mud all over my face. A horse galloped around the mountain path, a steel covered rider wielding a sword. My face hardened as I straightened, no fear on my youthful features. But I didn't stand a chance against the mounted rider.

I couldn't help the sharp intake of breath as the rider's sword separated my head from my shoulders. Ares made a strangled sound, and the image changed again. This time I was dressed as a maid, busy with a duster in my hand. I watched, barely breathing, as flames burst to life on the snow, and painfully slowly consumed the apparition of me.

"No," Ares choked.

The image changed yet again, and like a fucked up time-line of human history I watched myself die over and over, in a different time and place.

My mind couldn't turn the images into sense, couldn't process what it meant.

"What is this?"

"I couldn't kill you. The oracle said I had to kill you to get my true immortality, but something stopped me. So I sent you away from Olympus so I didn't have to share my power. And... And instead of you dying at my hand, you died a thousand times over in the mortal world." His voice cracked on the last word, and intense pain rocked through our connection, causing my own eyes to fill with burning tears.

This was what Ares had done that he couldn't tell me.

And now, on this mountain, he was being forced to live his worst fear. Was it me finding out? Or was it having to see the consequences of his actions?

I stared mutely at the image before us, of me

bloodied and wounded, lying on a filthy bed in a torn old-fashioned dress. A small cat with amber eyes was curled up beside me as the life left my eyes.

Zeeva said she'd been with me longer than I knew. This was real. I'd lived a thousand lives I had no recollection of. Ares had banished me from the world I belonged to and I had lived an endless cycle of powerless, violence-filled lives instead.

I'd never fit in. And I never would have.

"You came back to get me when you needed your power. When Zeus took yours, you sought me out after thousands of years."

Ares' look was pure anguish as I spoke.

"But if that hadn't happened, I would still be there. Destined to die unhappy, only to start all over again. In a world I would never belong to, never find contentment or joy in."

A hot tear slid down my cheek. The thought of being trapped for an eternity in endless unhappiness made me feel sick. And the pain rolling from Ares straight into my gut made me unsteady. I couldn't sort through the emotions, couldn't put them in the right order. I couldn't work out what was important and what was beyond fixing or caring about. I watched as an ancient Egyptian man plunged a short knife into my chest behind Ares.

"I'm sorry," he said. Never had two words sounded more sincere, more loaded with truth. But they weren't sinking in, the revelation of the life I had lived taking up too much space in my head.

Neither of us saw the chimera until it pounced.

21

BELLA

Solid weight slammed into me. I registered pain in my thigh and shoulder, and then I was crashing through freezing snow. Red descended over my tumbling vision, and my surroundings slowed as my war-sight kicked in.

The chimera was rolling with me, the snow leopard head rearing back to snap. I jerked my head as our roll through the snow continued in slow motion, leaving me on top of the creature. I jumped, then screamed in pain as the muscle in my thigh felt like it was being torn from my body. I slammed back down onto the chimera, my leap thwarted.

Gasping for breath, I looked down at my leg. The snake's jaws were clamped firmly around it. Searing pain lanced through my other shoulder and I realized my distraction had cost me. The leopard head pulled back, a lump of my flesh hanging from its jaws.

Power surged through my body, pain turning lightning fast into fury. The image of me in the purple dress with an army at my back filled my mind, and I blasted as much of the rage as I could at the chimera, thrusting *Ischyros* toward its heart as we skidded across the mountain path.

It worked.

The chimera was thrown backward with more force than I thought was possible for me to possess, and I screamed again as the snake's jaws were ripped from my leg. I realized within a heartbeat though that I had made a mistake. The momentum created by hurling the thing away from me worked both ways, and I was flying backward at almost the same rate as the chimera.

As my back hit the ground I started to skid. I scrabbled in the snow, desperately trying to find anything to cling on to, vaguely aware of the chimera slamming into the steep mountainside. If the chimera had been thrown toward the mountain, that meant I was moving in the opposite direction. Toward the edge of the mountain path.

"Bella!" Ares' roar was deafening, then I hit something soft but firm, sending me skidding sideways. It was his barrier, I realized, recognizing it at once from when he used it to stop me falling.

Magic, you fucking idiot! You have magic!

Drawing on the well of power burning inside me, I threw up my own walls of air, all around me. With a painful slam, I hit the first one, then the second, before mercifully coming to a stop. I closed my eyes and let my head collapse onto the ground, sending my power immediately to my leg, trying to heal it. I didn't look at it. I knew it would be a mess.

"Bella! Are you alright?"

A snarl caused my eyes to snap open again. How the hell had the chimera survived hitting the mountain that hard?

Sitting up as fast as I could, I scanned the mountain path but it was hard to see more than a few feet through the blizzard. I could see the golden glow of Ares though.

"Ares?" I yelled, then my heart leaped in my chest as he burst toward me, a chimera swiping at his golden armor. But this chimera had a red snake for a tail. It was a different one.

More snarls sounded, growing louder, and my heart began to thud against my ribcage. Ares swung with his sword, causing the red tailed creature to back off just a fraction, as at least six more prowled into view through the blizzard. They all walked low to the ground, shoulders rocking as they advanced. Ready to pounce.

I glanced at my thigh, already knowing I wouldn't be able to stand. Bile rose in my throat at the sight. I could see bone. My magic was strong enough to block most of the pain, but it couldn't heal my leg in time for me to fight.

Fear crept over me, starting in my chest and working outward, an icy dread tingling through my limbs and taking over my head.

"Ares!"

One of the creatures leaped at him, followed immediately by a second. "Ares!" He had his shield up, and was moving fast, landing blow after blow on the huge creatures, but there were six heads with vicious teeth and horns, and only one of him. A third joined the fight.

"I will not take your power! You need it to heal!" the God of War yelled as he ducked and dodged, keeping himself between me and the pack.

I tried to stand, using my sword to push myself up, but my useless leg gave out before I even got halfway.

Frustration escaped me in a roar.

He couldn't beat them alone. And certainly not if he wouldn't take my power.

"You must! Take it and defend us!"

He didn't answer, couldn't answer, as another chimera joined the fray, snapping at his feet.

Fury at being able to do nothing was gripping me, and I tried once more to stand, without using my damaged leg at all. With the help of my blade I managed to get to one knee, but my elation was short lived.

There were too many for Ares to keep back, and I barely had time to throw up my shield before a chimera leaped for me.

Unlike before, I only skidded for split second, knocked backward by the creature's strength. By the time I realized what had happened, it was too late.

I felt an almost detached numbness as I felt the ground beneath me disappear, and heard an animalistic shriek from the chimera as it too realized what was happening.

I was falling. Falling through empty air, nothing but snow around me. I would survive the fall. But Ares would die at the jaws of the chimera. At the thought of his face I felt a surge of agony through our bond, and fear for his life swamped me.

Instinctively, I began to push my power toward the bond, trying to force it to leave my body, to reach him. Everything I had learned about him, my past, what he had done to me became meaningless at the notion of losing him.

For a heartbeat I thought it was working. I could feel the power leaving my body, the connection flaring.

But then I hit the ground.

22

BELLA

I awoke with a jolt of fear, and flashing stars of light crashed across my vision as I sat up gasping.

"I'm alive." The shocked words came out as a croak, which turned into a wail as the pain hit me.

My leg. I looked down, fighting nausea at the sight of the gaping wound. I shut my eyes and sucked in air, trying to gather my scattered thoughts, trying to focus. Everything was hazy, memories and emotions charging around in my head like unleashed animals, and my body half numb and half ablaze with pain. It was as though my leg was taking up so much of my physical awareness that everything else had lost sensation.

Get it the fuck together, Bella. First things first, where am I? And where is Ares?

I opened my eyes and looked everywhere but my injured leg.

It was dark, but I could see enough to establish that I was in a cell.

Panic coiled tight around my chest as the realization that I was some sort of prisoner settled in. I tried to move, and a rattling sounded. "Oh god." My wrists were manacled. The pain from my leg was so bad it had blocked out the fact that I was fucking chained up. I lifted my manacled hands to my head desperately, the chain pulling.

My helmet was gone. And so was *Ischyros*.

"No, no, no." I could feel the panic spiraling, fear and confusion building. But no power came with it. No red mist, no surging strength. Ares had told me about manacles that stopped magical powers being used. He'd said they could be used on the demon.

But he'd also said only the three brothers, Zeus, Hades and Poseidon could use them. Surely that meant that they couldn't be those ones?

I gasped for breath, fighting to get control of myself. I could feel my burning ball of power, hot and ready under my ribs. It was still there. I tried to send it to my leg, to heal the debilitating pain. But nothing happened.

Find Ares. Memories of the mountainside tumbled through my mind, bitter resentment flashing to life in response to seeing my own death played out over and over again...

"Not now, Bella," I hissed aloud. "More important shit to deal with."

I needed to know where I was, and who had chained me up. That was my most immediate problem. That and the wound on my leg.

Surroundings first, I thought, still resisting seeing how bad the injury was.

I was sitting on a wooden floor, and the walls on three sides of the small room were also paneled in wood. The last wall was a series of tall iron bars. Cell bars.

Slow recognition dawned on me as I stared at the paneling. I'd seen it before, in the room full of stone tables.

I was on the demon's ship.

How was that possible? I was supposed to be in the Ares Trials! Nobody was supposed to interfere with them!

Fresh fear gripped me, but this time for Ares. It was instinctive, and it drowned out the turmoil of what I had recently learned about him. Whatever the hell had happened in the past, I knew I didn't want him dead. Bile rose in my throat at the thought and I searched inside myself for the connection to him. Hera had confirmed what I already knew, that there were two separate links between us. The one that had been there from the start, the one that I felt tugging when he used my power was lifeless, the distance between us too great for it to work. But the other, the one that had blossomed later and carried his emotions, his presence, his very essence to me was the one I sought.

A weak spark of anguish rolled through me, and I knew it wasn't my own. Ares was alive. But far, far away.

With a surge of relief, I tried again to summon my power, finally forcing myself to look at the bite in my thigh. The blood had congealed, so I was in no immediate danger from blood loss, but it was fiercely hot to touch, and many layers of muscle and flesh were visible above the sliver of pale bone. There was no way I'd avoid an infection. *That's if it's not already poisoned.* I knew from my previous experience with the manticore that creatures in Olympus had many other nasty ways of killing, in addition to all the teeth and claws.

When my healing power didn't respond, I tried to summon a fireball, but nothing happened. Impotent rage was building inside me the longer I attempted, and failed, to use the burning energy trapped in my body. It was all I could do not to start screaming in frustration.

I'd spent my entire life feeling like I was going to explode from the inside out. Like a person ten times larger than me was trying to bust out of the body it was trapped in.

And I now suspected I had spent many, many lives feeling like that. With nothing but pain to distract me, Ares' revelation wormed its way through my other thoughts, demanding my attention.

How many lives had I lived? It didn't surprise me that so many of them had ended violently. The need for confrontation was part of me. Had I got better at controlling it each time I was born into a new life?

Zeeva had told me that over the years my power had seeped out of me and into my blade. I felt a bone-wrenching pang when I thought about *Ischyros*. But her words made sense now. The power had left me and stored itself in the weapon over thousands of years, not just this short life-span.

Ares did this to me. His pain-filled words on the mountain came back to me. *"Instead of you dying at my hand, you died a thousand times over."*

But I remembered none of those deaths. In fact, dying repeatedly was not what made my heart wrench with betrayal. Instead, it was the knowledge that every time I started again would be just as awful and unfulfilling as the last. It was the thought of living the same miserable fucking life over and over that made hot fury and resentment boil under my skin. He had chosen to trap me in an endless cycle of misery.

Could I forgive him that?

Would I rather he had killed me in the first place?

No. I'm here now. And he loves me.

I knew he loved me. There was no way the Ares who had stood before me on the mountain would make the same decision now. He had planned to tell me the truth. After the Trials. He had planned to face his fear of me finding out, and the consequences that had carried.

But he had taken from me my life in Olympus, my power, and whatever family I might have had. He must have known I would never belong in the mortal world. Did he know how truly trapped and unhappy I would be, forever? Worse, his motivation had been greed. Desire for strength and power, pure and simple.

I ground my teeth and fell back onto the planks, my shoulder and leg pounding with pain, and frustration and sadness threatening to overwhelm me.

I had never felt anything like what I felt for Ares. I was bound to him, in a way that went beyond anything tangible. My soul, as old and fucked up as it apparently was, was connected to the God of War in a way I knew could never be undone.

I had lived most of this life at least, clinging to the belief that a person could change, could make mistakes and come back from them. If we couldn't be forgiven for our fuck-ups, then I was a lost cause. I needed to believe in forgiveness, for my own sanity.

But could I forgive him?

Ares was not the same man who had sent me to endure that shitty existence any more, was he?

The next time I woke, it was to a clear, cheerful male voice.

"Breakfast?"

I sat up quickly, managing to suppress the groan of pain this time.

The raging anger had kept me awake for as long as my body could take it, but the fall from the mountain had won out and eventually I had shut down completely. No dreams had disturbed me, and I had no idea at all how long I had been asleep for. My body ached from being on the wooden planks, though the discomfort was barely noticeable over the throbbing from my leg. I did think it was slightly less than the first time I woke up though.

"Who are you? Why am I here?" I shouted, blinking in the gloom.

Light gently pierced the darkness though the cell bars, making my eyes water.

"I thought you might like something to eat." Pain's handsome face came into focus on the other side of the bars. He was wearing Erimosian style clothes and a massive grin.

"What the fuck is going on? Why am I not in the Trial?"

"You lost, little goddess." Excitement danced through his dark eyes.

"What?"

"You didn't get to the top. You fell off the mountain, and Ares was overtaken by the chimera when he lost access to your power."

"Is he hurt?"

"Yes. He will probably die within the next few hours." Pure delight was written all over his face, and white-hot fury clawed up my chest.

"If he dies I swear to fucking god-"

Pain cut me off. "You can do nothing, little goddess. When he dies, you will become the new God of War. And Terror made a deal. If Ares lost the Trials, we get the God of War."

"You're- you're taking me in his place?"

"Of course. What would we want with a dead god?"

"The other Olympians won't let him die," I said desperately.

"The other Olympians have no choice. He took part in the Trials willingly and he was fully aware of the risks. And besides, he is useless to them now; he has no power. You have it all."

I felt sick as I stared at the gleeful Lord. My head was swimming, unable to believe his words. "He's a god. He can't die."

"No. You two combined are a god. The power only needs one of you. Now, do you want this food?"

"Go to hell," I spat. "Where is Ares?"

"Far from here, and beyond your help." His eyes flicked to the manacles on my wrists.

"What are these?" I shook them at him. Fear and anger was building in such a crescendo inside me that I was barely aware of my actions.

"They are what will stop you from saving him," he smiled. Bending, he set the tray down on the floor in front of the bars. "Terror will come and get you when Ares has finally given up his fight with death. We are expecting a visitor, and when they arrive you will need to be presented to them."

With a last fucked up grin, he turned and left, taking the light with him.

A desperate noise escaped my throat as I reached inside myself for the connection to Ares. Fear gripped me even tighter as I remembered what Hera had said. *Distance didn't weaken the bond between our souls.* The realization made tears fill my burning eyes. The connection was so weak because Ares was weak. In a rush of certainty, I knew Pain was telling the truth.

Ares was dying.

23

BELLA

Any doubt I had that I could forgive Ares was swept away by a tidal wave of emotion so intense I thought it might actually burst from my chest.

He couldn't die. He couldn't.

I loved him, and I couldn't handle the thought of a life without him. He was a part of me, and my life wouldn't be worth living with a hole that size in my heart.

The rational part of me that knew it was fucking absurd to feel so strongly, that I barely knew him, that all my survival instincts were clearly whacked, was silent.

I had to save him.

I shook my wrists as hard as I could, as tears spilled from my eyes. The roiling mass of power was desperate to escape me, but no matter how hard I tried to force it out, it remained trapped inside.

I needed to get to Ares, I needed to give him my immortality.

A sob clawed its way up my throat.

I needed to save his life.

I sought our bond, trying to feel for him. It was even weaker than before, an anguished pain coming from him that caused more tears to burn down my cheeks.

It wasn't physical pain that he was feeling, I realized. It was what he had done to me that was causing him the hurt.

"It's OK," I said aloud, squeezing my eyes closed and clenching my fists in helpless despair. "I forgive you, Ares. You should have taken my power. You should have taken it on the mountain." My voice cracked, more sobs taking over as I tried stupidly to force my power toward him. "You should have taken it," I cried, the heat inside me unbearable, the void I knew I faced without Ares torture to consider.

I felt a pull in my gut, and my sobbing stuttered. "Ares?" The pull got harder, the power connection flaring into life. "Ares!"

I poured power into the bond with everything I had, the burning, boundless ball of energy shrinking fast as I forced every ounce to Ares, to save his life.

It wasn't until there was nothing left burning in my chest at all that I felt the connection cut off abruptly. As though coming out of a trance, I started in surprise. I'd given him everything. He had all of my power. That had to be enough to save him, to make him immortal again. *It had to be.*

Slumping back onto the planks, I let the tears come, this time fueled by relief. He would survive. He had to survive.

I was not a person who ever really allowed myself to cry, but once the tears had started, I couldn't stop them. I realized I was crying for everything I had endured since coming to Olympus. It was as though all the good and all the bad had rolled together and was spilling out of me in a tidal wave of emotion. I cried for the pain and betrayal and frustration I had experienced, but I also cried for the sheer joy of falling in love with Ares. I cried with gratitude because I knew that even if I died now, I had experienced his love. I cried because I missed him already, because I needed him there beside me. And I cried because I couldn't bear the thought of losing him.

After what seemed like an eternity, I mercifully cried myself into a long and dreamless sleep, until a bang resounded through the darkness. I sat up, alert instantly. Just the act of lifting my body was hard. Without the ability to use my power I was weak and tired. But Ares had my power now. He would come, and it would be my turn to be rescued.

"I don't know what you did, but it would appear that I underestimated the strength of both your power and your feelings. And the manacles' effect on internal magical bonds."

Icy tendrils worked their way down my body as I recognized the voice. Light exploded through the cell, making me flinch and causing yet more liquid to leak from my eyes.

I gritted my teeth and spoke as a figure stepped up to the cell bars. "People have a habit of underestimating me, Aphrodite."

"I have to get to her!"

"You will be no use to her in this state. You must rest."

"Mother, let me go!"

Hera glared down at me, her magic pinning me to the lavish bed I'd awoken in. Bella's power poured through my veins, knitting my torn skin back together and filling my body with life-preserving strength and vitality. She was too far away for me to access her power though, and I didn't know how she'd sent me it. At first I'd feared the worst - I knew I'd get her power the moment she died. But I could feel her presence through the bond between our souls. She was angry and frustrated and scared, but she was alive.

"Ares, if you go to her before you are healed, then her sacrifices, and yours, will have all been in vain." Hera, Queen of the Gods and my mother, let out a long sigh before sitting down on the silk sheets beside me. "I am sorry, truly, that this is your burden to bear. But it will be worth it. The moment you are strong enough, I will help you to get to her."

I opened my mouth to shout and argue, but the sorrow in her eyes stalled me. She looked tired, I realized. And gods never looked tired. "Where have you been?"

"You will find out soon enough, I fear."

She was wearing a toga of bright teal, as she often did, but her usual opulent peacock feather headdress was absent, a simple crown in its place.

"The other gods have missed you," I said.

She gave me a wry smile. "I hope, son, that you are trying to tell me that you have missed me."

I glared at her. "Your counsel is honest. The Olympians need it."

The truth was, I did miss her advice. It was never directed explicitly at me - I did not have that kind of relationship with my mother. Heart-to-hearts were not something we had ever indulged in. I didn't think my father would allow it even if she or I had wanted to. But I found her presence a balm at the meetings of the gods. She was even and fair in most things, and fiercely loyal and vengeful in others. Exactly as she should be.

"I have not abandoned you," she said quietly. "I have been required to direct my power elsewhere, but I have done everything I can to ensure your safety."

I couldn't help the indignant snort escaping my mouth. "This is the first time I have seen you since Zeus stole my power! Until I found Bella, I was mortal!"

"And where did you get the idea to find her?"

I paused before answering. "A dream."

Hera nodded, her mouth a thin line. "Sent by me. And Bella's companion?"

"Your spy."

"For a very, very long time. I have been watching over that girl for centuries, once I found where you had sent her."

"Why?"

"Because the two of you are linked. You have been since you were born."

Slowly, Hera reached out, her finger brushing my cheek in the most matronly gesture she had made since I was a child. Flashbacks of her singing to me, smiling, and a feeling of actual love between us rolled through me, making my breath catch. "You know that my power is linked to marriage and true bonds. I am able to bond two people once they have found love with each other, but I am also able to feel the bonds that exist without my input. The ones created by magic or prophecy or true fate. That is what exists between you and Enyo. When the oracle told you that only one of you could be immortal while the other lived, you assumed it made her your enemy. When you went to kill her, you were both too young for the bond to have ignited. But I knew it was there, waiting. I stopped you that day. I sent the doubt that made you pause, that made you remove her from our world instead of killing her. I couldn't let you destroy the one thing in the world that could make you happy, even if it also had the risk of making you mortal."

I stared, wide-eyed. "You have known this my whole

life?" Hera nodded, eyes serious. "Why didn't you tell me?"

"You would not have believed me. You are as arrogant and stubborn as your father."

She was right, I realized, thoughts tumbling through my head. I would not have believed her. I had been certain Enyo was the one thing that could cause my death. I would never have believed that I was destined to love her.

"How were we bound?"

"Powers beyond my control or understanding. We do not know who birthed Enyo, only that it was a Titan. But her power is yours. When you shed Pain, Panic and Terror and removed their power from yours, they were shed from her too. You are a part of one another."

"I know," I breathed. I focused on my mother's face, and her expression softened just a touch. "I love her. And now I know that I have never loved before."

A smile took Hera's mouth, warm and at odds with the pain in her eyes. "A connection to somebody that runs that deep is the most joyous, and the most painful thing a being can experience."

"She knows what I did to her, yet she found a way to send me her power. She saved my life. Again. Even though I stole hers from her."

"Ares, it is only because of the life Enyo has lived in the mortal world that she is able to save you. Prophecy is a strange and often cruel thing. If she had not lived the life she has, she would not have become the Bella you have fallen in love with, the Bella who is morally good and forgiving. The Bella who can save you from the worst parts of yourself. If she had lived in Olympus, able to expend her power in the way you have, she would have ended up just the same as you."

"Then why couldn't I have been the one who had to die a violent death over and over, instead of her? Why couldn't I have been the one who had to become mortal to learn about forgiveness? I got to march around a glorious world, treated as royalty, while she suffered endlessly." My voice cracked, guilt swamping me as the images on the mountainside of Bella dying repeatedly played before me. "I would do anything to swap places with her. Anything."

"Son, she remembers none of those deaths. And Bella needs to be the person she is. It is what makes her strong. It is what brought the bond to life and made you fall in love with one another."

"I can't stand the thought of everything she has had to deal with, just so that she can come and save me from my own monster." The idea was unbearable.

"Ares, do not be so self-absorbed." Hera's voice was sharp, and I snapped my stinging eyes to hers.

"What?"

"Bella did not become who she is to save you; she became who she is to save herself. She is fierce and proud and strong because of it, stronger even than you. You want your chance to make amends? Well, now it is your turn to face adversity. It is your turn to save her."

25

BELLA

"Hera has just announced publicly that her son will survive. You had something to do with this." Aphrodite's eyes were hard as she stared down at me. She was fiercely beautiful, wearing the look of an ice queen. Her hair was as white as her skin, her lips and dress the color of blood.

"Fuck off, Aphrodite." I tried not to let my relief at her words show on my face as I spoke. *Ares was with Hera. He would be OK.*

The woman hissed at me. "You have no respect."

"I have plenty of respect, just not for petty, jealous assholes."

"I would not be so generous with my insults, if I were you. Three of Olympus' most unpleasant deities are willing to do my bidding."

"Ah, so you're going to threaten me with Ares' Lords of War instead of doing your dirty work yourself?" I narrowed my eyes at her. "Why are you here? What have you got to do with any of this? And where is Eris?"

"As if I'm going to tell you anything you want to know. All that is important is that you lost the Ares Trials. You belong to the Lords of War now. And they work for me." She leaned forward through the bars, a steely smile on her face as she whispered, "which makes you *mine*."

Being leered at through cell bars brought out the worst in me and I acted instinctively. I drew back my head, and spat at her.

The Goddess of Love shrieked as my saliva landed on her porcelain skin, and my lips quirked up into a smile, the dried tears on my cheeks cracking.

Then pain ripped through my wrists as I was lifted off my ass into the air, my body pulled to the extent of the chains attached to the manacles. They bit into my skin, blood welling instantly.

"You are a pathetic little brat," Aphrodite barked, wiping her perfect face. My body moved higher, and the manacles cut deeper. I tried to kick my legs but I was being pinned in the air by an invisible force.

"Why are you here?" I growled, refusing to show how much pain I was in.

"I am here because I am not fucking stupid, unlike that fool you have fallen in love with," she said, venom in her voice.

My mind whirred, trying to connect the dots. "Why would the Lords of War work for you?"

"They may be spirits of War, but they are hosted by men. And all men do exactly what I tell them to do." There was a note of smugness to her icy voice.

I blocked out the pain rolling in waves down my

arms and tried to follow my train of thought. The pieces tumbled into place in my mind. "You're working with Zeus."

She cocked her head at me. "Zeus is the most mighty of us all. Our true leader. Only a moron would fight against him."

"You mean Ares?"

She laughed. "And Hades and that idiotic water god, Poseidon. They're all fools. I found Zeus, despite him using the Guardian's power to mask himself. And I pledged my fealty to him and offered him my help. He is my true king. The Ares Trials were a gift to me to express his thanks. Zeus will not need the demon much longer, as he will have no need to hide from the other gods when his plan is complete. So, when Ares was sent to find the demon, I saw an opportunity to relieve some of my boredom. What could be more entertaining than watching a powerless, overgrown god defeated by his own underlings? I approached the Lords of War and told them to find Ares and offer him the demon if he underwent a series of Trials that would show the world how powerless he was."

"You weren't expecting my power, then," I said, rage lacing my voice. "And when we started winning, you cursed us instead."

Dark shadows swirled through the goddess' eyes. "You made a fool of me, and that can not be tolerated."

"When we broke your curse, you got Terror to up the stakes. Forcing Ares to commit his own being to the outcome." Fury was helping to block the pain, and my disgust for Aphrodite dripped from my words. "You used Ares like a fucking toy for years, then ruined his life when he didn't want you any more. You're worthless scum."

I jerked hard against the manacles as my body was pulled toward the bars, and I couldn't stop the cry of pain as the metal tore further into my skin.

"You have no idea what I am," Aphrodite hissed. "And you have no idea what Zeus is capable of. I am on the right side of the war that is coming, and I am stronger than them all. How I treat my toys is going to become your whole life, little brat. I own you."

The power holding me up vanished and I crashed to the floor. The pain from my wounded thigh as I hit the planks was blinding, the whole world flashing between black and bright white as my brain seemed to tip upside-down. For a moment I was sure I'd throw up. Dim light crept back into my vision as I gasped for breath and I clutched at the floor, waiting for the dizziness to abate.

When I finally trusted myself to move without puking, Aphrodite was gone.

"Bella?"

The voice dragged me from turbulent dreams filled with death and blood and darkness.

"Bella, wake up."

"Fuck off."

I lifted my manacled arms, trying to wrap them around my pounding head and shut the voice out. To shut everything out. It was all too dark and hazy.

Exhaustion had taken me completely. With no power left burning inside me, and *Ischyros* gone, I felt as weak as a kitten. The wound on my leg was sapping my human strength by the minute and the pain had numbed alarmingly in the last couple of hours. I knew that if I could no longer feel it, I was in trouble.

"Don't speak to me like that." The voice snapped, and I paused, recognizing it through my fog of fatigue.

"Zeeva?"

"Yes." I groaned as I moved my arms. They fell weakly to my sides as I tried to sit up.

Aphrodite's visit had left its mark. The skin on my wrists was shredded and bloody. "Are you here on the ship?" There was a note of hope in my dry, scratchy voice. I was painfully thirsty.

"I'm here." I squinted toward the bars, and saw a lithe little cat squeeze between them in the gloom. She was dragging something in her mouth. "I am sorry. About what happened on the mountain."

"Wasn't your fault," I croaked. Excitement and hope was forcing some energy into my limbs. If Zeeva was here, she could help me. If she had come from Hera, maybe it meant Ares was on his way too.

"Eat this." She rolled the thing she was dragging toward me. It looked a little like an orange, and I winced as the manacles moved against my cuts when I picked it up. "It will help."

I didn't question the cat, and began peeling the skin off what I assumed was a fruit. "Where is Ares?"

"I do not know."

Alarm skittered through me. "I thought he was with your master, Hera?"

"Then you know more than I do. I was under Terror's enforcement longer than I needed to be." Her usually haughty voice was laced with fury.

"He only just let you go?"

"Yes. And he will regret doing so."

"Wait, you just got free and you're here? Instead of with Hera?"

"Before I was freed I heard Pain say that they had you on the ship, and that it was moored off the north coast of Pisces. I should have gone back to my master but... I was worried."

"About me?"

"Yes."

Despite my increasingly shit situation, I beamed. "I knew it! I knew you loved being my cat!"

"I am not your cat. But... I am your friend. Terror was able to take control of me for the purposes of the Trial, but he should never have been able to hang on to my power for as long as he did. The Lords are powerful. Too powerful. Somebody is helping them."

"Aphrodite is working with them and Zeus," I told her, before putting a segment on the orange-thing in my mouth. Delicious tangy liquid instantly coated my tongue, and a out-of-place cheerful feeling spread through me. "What is this?"

"Portokali. It will help with the fatigue. That makes

sense about Aphrodite. Hera knew that one of the Olympians was helping Zeus. I do not think she suspected her though."

"She's a coward and an asshole."

"The Goddess of Love is no coward. She is smart and manipulative and ambitious."

"She is a coward," I insisted. "She won't fight me. She keeps storming off."

"Her powers do not tend toward fireballs and super-strength like yours."

"How do I defeat her?"

"You can't. She is one of the strongest gods. There is little more powerful than love. And if she is truly working with Zeus, then your only chance at getting back to Ares is to run."

"Run? I don't walk away from a fight, and that woman needs a fucking beating. And I'm fed up of being told I can't defeat my enemies."

Zeeva sauntered up closer, then bared her needly teeth as she saw the manacles. "I'm pleased to see your fighting spirit is returning. But you will need it to escape, not aggress. Zeus must indeed have been here. Only the three brothers can use these manacles."

"Zeeva, I can't run even if I wanted to. My leg is useless."

"At some point they will have to take the manacles off. Then you flash."

"I have no power. Even without these evil freaking cuffs."

"What?"

"I sent it all to Ares. He needed the immortality."

Zeeva blinked slowly, and I put more portokali in my mouth. "You... you are mortal right now?"

"Yeah. Hundred percent human. And it sucks. Of all the ways to die, a big fucking hole in my leg was not the glorious ending I'd hoped for."

"How did you send Ares your power if he is in Hera's realm?"

"I don't know. I just did. I gave him everything."

"You love him? After what he did to you?"

"Completely."

There was a long silence, only broken by the sound of my chewing on the fruit. I knew, somewhere inside myself, that giving up my only chance of escape from this place to save Ares life was, well, crazy. But it hadn't been a choice. I hadn't weighed up options and reached a balanced, well-informed conclusion.

I had given him everything because that was what I had to do. Picturing his face made my chest ache, and it was nothing to do with my poor state of health. I longed to see him. To touch him, to kiss him.

"He will come for you." Zeeva said the words with certainty, and hope fired through my shattered body.

"I don't know if he will be strong enough. He very nearly died. And this wound is taking more from me every hour."

Zeeva moved cautiously to my leg, and sniffed her little cat nose. When she spoke, her tone was grave. "We must hope he makes a speedy recovery, and knows where to find you."

"Can you go to him? Tell him where I am?"

"I will leave at once."

There was a flash of teal, and when it faded I frowned. Zeeva was still sitting by my numb thigh.

"Err," I said. "I thought you were on your way to my rescuer?"

"The ship will not allow me to flash." The fury was back in her voice, and in the gloom I saw her eyes blaze dangerously.

The glimmer of hope I'd felt oozed out of me. "Shit."

"Indeed."

I blew out a sigh, and ate more portokali. "Zeeva, how did I send my power to Ares with the manacles on?"

"They must only block external magic."

"Oh. Another question, as you're stuck with me. Can you give me back those memories you told me about?"

"You saw how most of them ended already," she said quietly. "But I can tell you some of the happier ones."

"Do you know who I was before I was sent to the mortal world?"

"Many years ago, when the Titans who had helped Zeus become king had all disappeared, Zeus wanted all the Titan descendants rounded up. Hecate, who helps Hades rule the Underworld and is one of the most powerful remaining Titans in existence, tried to get to them first. She found you and a few others who were as powerful as the Olympians, and convinced the gods to let you learn your powers peacefully."

"Do you think she created the bond between me and Ares?"

"No, she's not really... loving or maternal. She is the Goddess of Ghosts."

"Oh."

"Hera championed you as the Goddess of War when it emerged how strong your power was, and how closely linked with Ares' own it appeared to be. When you disappeared, most people believed Zeus had something to do with it, due to his hatred of Titans. When he was accused, he had a fit of rage and removed all memory of a Goddess of War from everybody. Except his wife and Ares."

"Huh. So, I guess I still don't have a family."

"You have Ares. And... I suppose you have me."

26

BELLA

The scant energy I gained from Zeeva's portokali kept me awake for another half hour or so, during which I held the image of Ares, assured and calm, in my mind.

He would come for me. He would heal fast with all the power, and would find me. Somehow.

The strange thing was, I wasn't actually afraid of dying. Now that the flood of tears and overwrought emotion had been allowed the escape my body, I was *angry*.

I had finally discovered the truth about my past, the reason I was such a misfit, such a freak. And even better than that, I'd found somebody that understood me. It would be too damn cruel to find Ares, then lose him like this, so soon. It wasn't fair, and the idea of never seeing his face again filled me with hatred for the people who had done this to us.

Hatred for Aphrodite, mostly.

She had been furious that I'd managed to save his

life. She'd wanted him to die. If I succumbed to my wounds in the shitty cell, at least I had saved Ares, I thought, drawing comfort from the knowledge.

I had saved him. Nothing was more important.

"Bella?"

A bubble of air in front of me shimmered and the voice was coming from it. And it was loud. Loud enough that I cried out in surprise. "Eris?"

"Oh thank fuck for that, I thought I was out of power completely. Listen to me, do not interrupt and do not fucking say no."

I opened my mouth to answer her, but she continued speaking before I could.

"That mother-fucking bitch has trapped me in the mortal world, and she's muted my power. I've got fuck all left, and what little I did have, I used saving my brother's sorry ass."

"What?" I couldn't help the interruption. What the hell was she talking about?

"He's my brother, I'm connected to him. I felt his death starting, even from here. I couldn't heal him from so far away, but your bond to him is epic, so I used what power I had left to amplify that instead."

"You're the reason I could give him my power from so far away?"

"Yeah. And I knew it would be difficult but I didn't know it would drain me almost completely. Must be those stupid fucking manacles you have on. I have no way to recharge here. Aphrodite has made sure of that. This is the last time I'll be able to talk to you, and I'm calling in every fucking

favor you and Ares owe me. Get me the fuck out of the mortal world."

"We will. I swear, we will. But... I'm not really in a position to help right now," I said, slowing down as I finished the sentence.

"Well, fucking get into a position where you can!"

"Aphrodite has me trapped, I'm mortal, and I've got a fatal wound. Unless Ares gets here soon, I'm dead or spending eternity as her plaything."

"Ares will come for you. He'd better fucking be coming for you."

"He will," I nodded, even though I assumed she couldn't see me. "We'll find you, I promise. Are you in any immediate danger?"

"I'm in immediate danger of having no power and being bored to fucking death. I'm an ancient, all-powerful deity. This is not how I want to live my life."

Relief that she was safe mingled with the suffocating memories of living in a world that was so utterly wrong for you. I knew how shit that was. But, she would be fine for a while at least.

"I'm sure you'll be perfectly good at causing chaos without any power," I told her.

She snorted mentally. *"Come and find me, Bella. Do not leave me here."*

"We will. If we survive this, we will. And, Eris... Thank you. For saving his life."

I slept fitfully for what could have been an hour or five - I had no idea. When I awoke, I could sense a presence around me, but my body was too broken to react. I was sprawled on the planks, and I couldn't feel the wound on my thigh at all anymore. I tried to lift my head to look at it, but it was as though my skull weighed as much as my old punch-bag.

"Aphrodite?" I tried. Somebody was in the cell with me, I was sure.

"You're mortal. You don't need these any more."

The voice was male and unfamiliar, but as I felt the manacles slip from my wrists I realized who must have spoken.

"Zeus?" I moved my hands tentatively. The torn skin hurt as I moved my wrists, but I was grateful that the heavy feeling was gone from my arms. I tried again to lift my head.

If Zeus was really here, I wanted to see him. To speak to him.

"I have never seen my son like this. You have had quite an effect on him." The words were deep and lyrical, and an awestruck feeling threatened to overtake me as I struggled into a sitting position. My head was swimming, my insides unsteady. A well built man was standing over me, with dark hair shot through with gray. When my vision swam into focus for a few brief seconds I could see that his eyes shone purple.

I needed to worship this man. He was the king of the gods, most powerful being in Olympus. He was strong and beautiful and regal.

"My king," I rasped.

"How did you do it? How did you best Aphrodite and save him?"

Zeus' words floated into my addled brain, and I tried to make sense of them. How did I save him? "Save who?"

"My son. Ares. The God of War."

Ares' face filled my mind, blasting out the confusion like dynamite. Anger flooded my system, and I put my hands flat on the planks beneath me to steady myself. "You were going to let him die," I hissed. "You were going to let Aphrodite kill your son."

"Ares is his own man. It is not my responsibility to take care of him. Particularly when my efforts have been so consumed elsewhere." There was a bitterness to his voice that made me even more angry.

"But he is only vulnerable because of you! You stole his power!"

"He committed treason." The god's seductive tone had hardened, and I heard a rumble of thunder in the distance. "He tried to get in my way, and he paid the price."

"He tried to stop you unleashing a monster into the world."

"He is a fool. He can't see past the tired rhetoric of my narrow-minded brothers," Zeus hissed, and suddenly he was inches from my face. "I don't know how you seduced him away from Aphrodite, and I don't care. But, I am glad that you will die in his place."

Before I could ask the snarling god anything else he was gone. Did that mean he was glad his son survived?

Did he feel anything at all for Ares? Or was he just trying to scare me?

"Asshole," I spat.

"It's not advisable to swear at deities like Zeus." Pain stepped out of the shadows, up to my cell bars. I looked around in the gloom for Zeeva, relieved that I couldn't spot her. It was best if nobody else knew she was here. It might give me an advantage.

"So you got him to take off the manacles for a reason, huh?" I tried to sound as casual as I could, even as my heart beat an increasingly irregular rhythm against my ribcage.

"Aphrodite wants to play with her new toy, and she doesn't like it down here. She's asked me to bring you up on deck." An evil glint shone in Pain's dark eyes, and I couldn't help the icy shudder from tracking down my spine.

It seemed that I had run out of time.

27

BELLA

Pain literally had to drag me up the narrow wooden steps that led from deep in the hull of the ship, where I had been imprisoned. My useless leg didn't hurt as it thumped against the steps. There was more light in the stairwells that we were moving through, and I could see now that the wound had gone a gross green color. It made me feel sick whenever I looked at it, so I tried not to. I made myself as heavy and awkward as possible, just to piss Pain off, and eventually he resorted to throwing me over his shoulder and carrying me down corridors and up staircases.

I didn't try to memorize the route we were taking, or work out an escape plan. My brain was too fuzzy, my body too tired. If I hadn't had the fruit Zeeva had given me, I'd probably have died from thirst already.

"How long have I been on the ship?" I asked. My throat hurt when I spoke, but it wasn't in me to keep quiet.

"A few days. Long enough."

Surely that was enough time for Ares to heal? Why hadn't he found me yet?

"If your bitch-mistress wants to keep me alive long enough to play with me, you're going to have to feed and water me. Humans need that sort of shit."

"Aphrodite knows what humans need. Don't you worry about it, ex-baby goddess."

He emphasized the word ex delightedly and I scowled at his back. They knew I was mortal now. He was right. I was an ex-goddess.

The light was so bright when we eventually emerged onto the deck that tears sprang to my eyes immediately. Pain dropped me unceremoniously onto the planks as I squinted around, pain jarring through me as I landed on the wood.

Pastel clouds surrounded us, and the epic solar sails hung from the masts, shining so brilliantly that they hurt to look at.

"That's a nasty looking wound." I peered blearily at Aphrodite. She had dropped the ice-queen look, and now had caramel colored skin and baby pink hair. She wore a black wrap-around dress and had full, sensuous pink lips and onyx eyes.

"Not as nasty looking as your face," I said, and gave her a sarcastic smile.

We both knew she was beautiful. But I doubted many people told her she wasn't, so I got a kick out of the words regardless.

She narrowed her eyes as her smile widened. "Oh yes. Yes, yes, yes. I can see why that oaf fell for you. I imagine that when you are together you are like immature teenagers, fighting and cursing like idiots?"

I shrugged from my half-sitting position on the deck. "Well, there's one thing we do better than teenagers do, and I can assure you it's not fighting."

Her features darkened momentarily. "You will never live up to me, little girl."

"Aphrodite, I don't need to live up to you. You and I are nothing alike. We are non-comparable."

"So you think Ares doesn't wish that you could make him feel like I can?" Her voice dripped with sex and seduction. And for a moment, I believed her. Doubt filled me. There was no way I could possibly be a lover like her, no way I could possibly make Ares feel as good as she could.

But then I remembered. *Ares loved me.* Ares was a part of me, and I him. We were meant to be together, destined for one another, and nothing in the world could come close to the feel of his skin against mine, his arms around me, his lips on mine.

"I don't need to have this conversation with you, Aphrodite. I'm done. Do whatever the fuck it is that you hauled me up here to do, give me some food and water, and send me back to that shitty cell, where I don't have to look at your ugly-ass face."

The goddess's eyes filled with fury, and she lifted her dainty arm, snapping her fingers. "Pain! She's all yours. Do not kill her though, or it will be the last thing that spirit of yours does in that body."

Pain stepped forward, a smile on his handsome face. "Of course, mighty one." I looked around myself as quickly as I could manage, my head spinning as soon as I moved it too fast.

Panic was leaning against the railings to my left, and Terror was behind me, standing by the main mast. There was no sign of the Underworld demon. Or Zeeva.

Mortal or not, I had enough years of training for my fight-or-flight instincts to kick in. Ninety-nine times in a hundred, they told me to fight. But I had nothing in the tank. I was empty.

I hadn't given up hope that Ares would come, but I wasn't naive enough to think there was a way out of whatever was in store for me right now.

Neither fight, nor flight, was an option. So the next best thing was to give my attackers nothing. No satisfaction, no reason to come after me again. That was how bullies were dealt with, that was how to bore somebody who went after an opponent who couldn't fight back, or win. Give them nothing.

Pain's eyes roared to life with a burning yellow as he thrust his hand out. My body lurched off the planks as though tied to him by a tether, and I flew up into the air just as I had when Aphrodite had visited me in the cell. I closed my eyes, concentrating on slowing my racing heart, but I didn't have time to take the deep breath I wanted to.

White hot fire exploded to life in my thigh, as

though all the numbness had been expelled completely. Sheer agony shot in waves up my leg, smashing into the base of my spine and then shooting up into my skull like electric shocks.

Nothing had ever hurt like it, and I couldn't suck in breath, couldn't make a sound, the pain was so consuming. Darkness and stars descended over my vision and before I could work out how to breathe again, I blacked out.

"She's mortal, you fucking idiot. If you hit her with that much, her body will just shut down."

"I forgot. Do you know how long it's been since I tortured someone completely mortal? They tend to stay out of my way these days."

I could hear Pain and Panic talking as I came round, but I didn't dare open my eyes. Aftershocks of pain were still racing up my back from my leg, but mercifully most of the numbness had returned. I felt sick, but I knew there was nothing in my system to bring up.

My head lolled and my chin hit my chest. I realized foggily that I was still being held up in the air.

"Let me have a go. At least I can't accidentally knock her out." Panic's voice brimmed with excitement and my stomach clenched.

I was trapped. Their plaything to torture as they pleased. And there was no way for me to fight back or escape.

"Fine. But I want another go before she goes back to the cells."

"Deal."

I heaved to the left suddenly, before jerking back to the right. Panic was shaking me.

"Wakey, wakey!"

My eyes fluttered open and as soon as Panic came into focus, I forced a laugh to my lips. They may have had me as helpless as a kitten, but I wasn't going to let them see my fear.

"You think this is funny?" Panic cocked his head at me.

"No, not this," I rasped. "I'm picturing Ares tearing you limb from limb when he gets here, his power fully restored. It's a highly entertaining image."

"You know, you're just like us? Made of the same thing. You enjoy seeing others in Pain, enjoy seeing their Panic, enjoy instilling Terror in them."

"You misunderstand me," I told him, using most of my energy to hold my head up so that I could look him in the eye. "I find the idea of *you* experiencing those things most enjoyable. But that's because you're a complete fucking asswipe. I'm not a fan of nice, normal folk being terrorized. Just total fucktards like you three."

Panic snarled, and then I was flying through the air, toward the railings of the ship. My body lurched to a stop as I reached them, and my stomach seemed to jump into my throat as I tilted forward, forced to look straight down over the edge of the ship. I could see land, but only just, it was so far below us.

My mind filled abruptly with images, first of me falling from the mountain and the chimera shrieking, then of me hitting water and tentacles wrapping around me, dragging me under. I felt my body begin to tip, the images in my mind mingling with reality.

Then I was falling, the ship shooting past me as I dropped, the wind rushing against me and making my hair whip around my face. My chest was constricting, air was eluding me. No part of me wasn't sweating and fear was crawling its way up my throat, fighting for space with the panic.

There was a flash and then I was above the ship, near the top of the solar sails, still falling. Within seconds I smashed hard into the deck, pain rocking through my ribs as the wood splintered beneath me. I gasped for breath, rolling onto my uninjured side.

Panic's laughter carried across the deck, a feminine chuckle alongside it.

"How many times could you survive that fall, little girl?" Aphrodite asked.

"As many as it takes until Ares gets here," I panted, sucking in air.

"Let's see about that."

28

ARES

A roar of frustration escaped my throat, and I slammed my fist down on the marble table. It cracked, shattering onto the white tiles below.

My strength was back, in full force. All the power that had been stolen from me and I had yearned for so hard was returned.

And I didn't care.

"Ares, if you are going to act like a child then do it elsewhere! I am trying to find Bella and you are not helping."

I bared my teeth at my mother before I could stop myself. She had been standing over the table for what seemed like an eternity, a portal shimmering over it, but it had vanished with my outburst. Hera glared back at me from under her freshly-donned elaborate peacock headdress, her gaze filled with authority.

Whirling away, I stamped toward the edge of the temple and glared out over the forestland surrounding us, trying to keep my temper from brimming over its too-small container. "I will rip them apart, limb from limb."

"I'm sure you will, if we ever find them." Hera's voice dripped with annoyance.

The only reason I could keep any calm about myself at all was the fact that I knew Bella was still alive. I could just feel her through our connection. It was weak, and growing weaker, but she was a fighter. As my mother had said, she was stronger than I was. She would never give in.

But she was mortal now. I had every ounce of her power, I could feel it. Which meant there was a limit to her ability to fight the Lords of War.

If another Olympian was there, as my mother seemed to think there might be, then Bella did not stand a chance. The thought flashed into my head and rage welled through my center, flooding my muscles and making me swell.

"For the sake of Olympus, Ares, will you go somewhere else so I can work in peace!"

I had finally cracked Hera's patience. I threw her another angry glare as I stamped down the steps of the temple and out into the forest. I let my body grow with power as I went, trying to take some comfort in the return of the ability. But I got none. What was the use in being huge and mighty and powerful, if it was without her?

The sound of wood cracking loudly in the distance made me pause in my furious march. The trees around me began to rustle. I looked over my shoulder at the temple, still only a few feet behind me, before pushing my power-enhanced senses out into the forest.

The second I did, Dentro materialized before me, his body seeming to melt out of the browns and greens until a fully-formed, enormous dragon's body wove its way amongst the dense foliage.

My body started to move automatically into its reflexive stance, sword drawn and chest squared, but then I slowed to a stop. Bella and this creature had become friends. She cared for it.

"Do you know where she is?"

"I do. It took me some time to find her, and I had some help, but I know where she is."

Hope, relief and pure happiness flushed the rage from my system in a heartbeat.

"Mother!" I yelled for Hera, then turned back to Dentro's massive face. "Let's go."

"Not so fast, Warrior God. Last time I saw you, you were trying to kill Bella. I have become inexplicably fond of that fierce little goddess, and now I sense that you have her power. All of her power."

"I can guarantee you, dragon, you are not as fond of Bella as I am." I snarled the words, feeling the rage returning. I would not be denied her now, not when I was so close.

"I require your assurance that you only have her best interests at heart."

"Her best interests are staying alive, you idiotic beast! She needs me, now!"

I had grown again, and my sword was clutched in both hands. My chest felt tight and the War power wasn't forcing out my emotions like it always used to. My adoration, fear and love for Bella was permanent.

"Would you die for her?"

"Yes." My reply was instant, loud and true.

Dentro nodded his huge wooden head once, then lifted it to look over my shoulder. I turned to see my mother standing at the temple edge, atop the white stone steps. She nodded at the dragon, then vanished in a flash of teal.

"We must go too, now! Where should I flash to?" Urgency made my words tumble together but the dragon understood me.

"Bella is on a ship, and flashing is not possible there. I will take you."

My mouth fell open slightly as the creature lowered its neck to the ground. A dragon allowing a being to ride it was unheard of. In response to my awe, Dentro spoke again. "I do this for her. Not for you. Never will you be offered my neck again." His voice was tight, and I moved quickly, before he could change his mind.

His bark-covered skin was rough, and I was grateful for my armor as I pulled myself into a sitting position at the base of his neck.

"Hold on, Warrior God," he said, and then we were launching into the sky.

"*I have found your helmet.*" Zeeva's voice cut through the whistling air as I fell.

The spark of hope her words caused was knocked from me completely as I slammed into the deck. Another of my ribs popped, and pain squeezed around my middle, suffocating me. I could hear myself wheezing, but I couldn't lift a limb, raise my head, or even move an inch. I just lay sprawled on the planks, trying to force enough air into my lungs to keep me alive a little longer. Until I could see Ares again. His face filled my mind, forcing out the doubt and fear.

"*Bella, do not give up now. If you can reach your helmet then they can't get into your head anymore.*"

They didn't need to get into my head. They were breaking my body. Even listening to her mentally was a mammoth effort. I had nothing left. My strength was utterly sapped.

"*Roll onto your back.*"

I knew that if I did what Zeeva said, I would be

flung up into the air again, then pitched over the edge of the ship, only to be flashed over the deck to land on the solid wooden planks.

"He is here."

This time the spark of hope was so big, nothing could put it out. My body tapped into a reserve of energy I didn't know I had, and I rolled, looking around desperately.

I instinctively felt for our connection and found it immediately, burning bright and hot.

It was true. *Ares was nearby.*

"Look up."

I realized at the same time Zeeva spoke that the Lords had stopped looking at me and were craning their necks to peer up into the clouds. There was a shape in the distance, a dark spot, small but growing. A moment later, I could make out massive wings. Green and brown wings.

And a tiny, brilliant golden light.

"Dentro found him." I breathed the realization a second before Aphrodite's heels clicked loudly on the deck.

"Terror," she barked. The marble man moved forward from the mast in response. "Let's make sure that Ares is given a formal welcome."

With a lurch I was dragged up into the air again. Being slammed repeatedly into the deck hadn't just broken a few of my ribs. My left wrist felt all kinds of wrong and my foot dangled at a weird angle on my numb leg.

I knew that I couldn't take much more. Everything

hurt beyond what I thought I was capable of bearing, and I was sure that the only reason I was still conscious was because my mind was so fixated on one thing.

Ares.

I tried to turn my head, to see his golden glow, and Terror laughed. The sound made the hairs on my skin stand on end.

Slowly, he rotated me to face the dragon, wings beating through the clouds toward us. Ares shone like a gleaming beacon on Dentro's back and love swelled through my body, a brief and blessed relief from the pain.

But as I watched, the dragon pitched hard to the left and the golden light that I knew was Ares slipped from his back.

"No!" My voice was barely audible as Ares began to plummet though the clouds. Fear for his life gripped me, and I had to force myself to stay calm. He was immortal. He had all the power. He couldn't die.

But I could. And if he didn't get here soon, I would.

His glowing body disappeared from view, and Terror chuckled as he turned me back to face him. "Stealth was never really the God of War's style," he said, sauntering closer. It was inexplicable how a featureless face could carry so much menace. The inky swirls crawled across the surface of the stone, dark and foreboding.

"He'll be back," I croaked.

"No doubt. And when he comes back, he'll fall into her arms, not yours." He nodded his head backward, to where Aphrodite stood with her arms folded, her curvaceous body glowing softly.

At first his words glanced straight over me. But then they seemed to permeate through my mind, settling where they shouldn't.

I knew, deep down, that Ares was mine. But... But what if he was right? What if Ares stood before the two of us and chose her?

"And then, when he is at his most vulnerable, she'll strike."

With a rush I saw an image, clear as day, of Aphrodite plunging a knife into Ares' chest. Blood the color of gold spilled from him, his face twisted into agony.

"No! No, stop!" If any part of me knew that what I was seeing was Terror's magical influence, it didn't register. I was too tired, too weak, too broken, to fight it, or even to understand it. The images took over and my brain accepted them.

The pain was worse than the broken bones, than the wound in my thigh. I was being torn open from the inside out.

"Terror!"

That voice...

I forced my streaming eyes open as I dropped once more to the planks. But I didn't feel a thing.

Dentro landed on the ship's deck, shrinking his huge body to fit, and Ares leaped from his neck as the whole ship shuddered. He was twenty feet tall at least, and his armor shone so bright I had to blink.

His fall from the dragon had been one of Terror's visions. My heart began to pound in my chest, I was so desperate to believe that Ares was really there, that he hadn't fallen.

His boots met the planks and then he was moving toward me, lightning fast. "You have taken your last breath, Terror," he roared as he reached my side, dropping to his knees. His armor clanked and I blinked again as he wrapped one arm beneath me, pulling me to him.

"Tell me I'm not dreaming," I whispered. I felt his anger radiating from him, tempered by the intensity of his tenderness.

"I am here, Bella. Take the power. Now." Heat flared to life in my gut and warmth began to spread through my body. There was a searing flash of pain in my thigh which made me cry out, but then the familiar tingles of the healing magic took over.

With terrifying slowness, Ares rose to his feet.

"You will pay for what you have done to her. With your life."

Bang. A drum beat so loud that the ship vibrated.

Terror hissed as golden light pulsed from Ares, tinged with red. Then the marble man began to rise into the air, just like I had over and over.

"Master, please-" Terror began, his scratchy voice no longer mocking and cool. He was scared. The spirit of Terror was scared.

Shakily, I got to my own feet, unable to put weight

on my leg, but gripping Ares' enormous arm to hold myself up.

Bang. A second drum joined the first. They began to beat together, the sound of clashing steel ringing in the air. Heat and the smell of sweat and iron and blood washed over the deck of the ship. My spine straightened, and my body began to swell.

Red descended over my vision as screams filled the air.

"Ready?" Ares said.

"Yes."

Together, we unleashed the power of War.

Terror screamed as a crack appeared in his pristine skull. It spread, slowly at first, then faster, tracing down his whole stone form. His scream cut off abruptly, and I felt the wave of power roll from us as his body froze for a split second. The drums beat faster, the chants of war and sound of explosions surrounding us completely.

"I told you Ares would fuck you up," I said, then he shattered.

A million pieces of marble showered the wooden planks, and I stumbled at the exertion of power. Ares caught me, pulling me close and staring into my eyes. Fire, bright red and orange, and full of the promise of life, flared in his eyes.

"You're really here. On dragon-back, glowing gold. An actual freaking knight in shining armor." I was half-laughing and half-sobbing.

"Did you think I wouldn't come?" Raw emotion flowed from him, straight into my own soul.

"I knew you would. I just... didn't know if you'd get here in time. It was getting hard to hold on."

Before he could answer me, Aphrodite's voice cut through the moment. "I'm so glad you could join us, Ares," she said, her voice venomous.

A gleaming golden shield shimmered into being around us and Aphrodite's tinkling laughter trickled through it. Ares lowered me gently to the planks, then leaped to his feet, putting himself between her and my still healing form. My ribs no longer hurt like hell but my legs weren't functioning properly and I was exhausted. But the healing magic was working, thank fuck.

"I don't know why you're doing this, Aphrodite, but enough is enough."

"She's working with your father," I said, my voice sounding stronger. I didn't want to draw too much power from him but it burned hot, calling to me.

"Why?"

"The same reason you should be working with him too. He is our king," Aphrodite drawled.

"I disagreed with his actions in the Underworld. What he did was reckless and wrong."

"It is not your place to disagree with his actions. It is your place to support and obey him. Pain, come here please."

I pulled harder on the magic connection, allowing

the molten pleasure of healing power to flood through my system faster.

The ship lurched and I looked over to see Dentro flying backward as a pink dome of light sprang up around us, encompassing the whole ship. The dragon, now on the outside of the shield, whipped his tail against it and bright fuchsia light sparked from the contact.

"That should keep the meddling beast out," Aphrodite muttered, before turning back to Ares. "You will regret coming here."

"Hand over the demon, and we will leave you and my father to whatever scheme you have concocted."

"No. I have never done as you have bid me, Ares, and I don't intend to start now." She cocked her head, her lips curving into a cruel smile. "I have to admit, I am sorry that I have lost my favorite trophy. The mighty God of War with his claws and fangs and pride was so much fun to play with."

I expected Ares to lose his temper at being mocked, but he was surprisingly calm when he answered her.

"Let it go, Aphrodite. You can't interfere with love like this, and you know it. We broke your curse. You are done. Move on."

Her face twisted, and it was the first time the woman hadn't looked drop-dead gorgeous. "I'm done when I say I am, you fool. You don't know what it is like to bear my burden, to watch as the world around me implodes and explodes on my cue. You don't know how the balance of my power works, what it does to my soul."

I'd never heard anybody speak with such bitterness, and for the first time, I actually considered what it might be like to hold the power of love. Until meeting Ares, I hadn't known its power. I'd seen it, on stage and on screen, I knew the rumors of its intensity. But I had never imagined it could invade every single atom of my being, or that it had the potential to truly change a person.

"I am done with this conversation," she snapped, whirling around. "I have suffered enough. When Zeus' plan comes together, none of this will be relevant. I do not need you, or the little brat, to enjoy his new world."

"New world? What are you talking about?"

"Zeus isn't taking your mutiny lying down. He is going to reward those who have remained loyal."

"What do you mean by new world?" Ares pushed.

"It does not matter what I mean. You will not be here to see it."

Before he could respond, a deafening crack of thunder echoed around us, and purple lightning split the sky as it darkened ominously.

I may not have been a native of Olympus, but even I knew what that meant.

Zeus was coming.

30

ARES

My father materialized on the deck of the ship before me, bolts of hissing lightning scorching the deck in a ring around him. He was trying to be intimidating. And succeeding.

I was partway to my knees before I could help it. The King of the Gods had a presence that went far beyond normal magic. It could not be resisted.

"Son. I see that taking your power from you has not made you any smarter."

"I see that you saw fit to hand it to a rogue demon," I answered, through gritted teeth.

Zeus looked as he often did, ten feet tall and strikingly good-looking, with silver and dark hair, bright purple eyes and a toga that barely hid his sculpted body. He looked as I had wanted to look most of my life.

"You were no longer suitable to hold the role of God of War."

Anger fired through me. "Cronos was imprisoned with the help of allies we no longer have! Letting him go free was an unwise risk, and as the God of War I am well versed in risks."

"You underestimate my might, little boy? You believe I am not strong enough?" Power crackled around the god, pain licking my skin as electricity hummed through the air. His purple eyes darkened as he grew even more in size, looming over everyone on the deck of the ship. I heard movement and glanced over my shoulder to see the remaining two Lords of War moving backward, eyes averted from the mighty king. Aphrodite, however, stayed where she was, a smug smile on her pristine face. "You do not believe that I could overpower that old Titan? Your lack of faith in my ability is treason," Zeus growled.

"Disagreeing with you is not treason. Nor is it a reason to strip me of my power." Bitterness laced my words.

"Treason is what I say it is. I am your king, whether you want me to be or not." Thunder rumbled in the distance with his words and the sky above us darkened. I could not reason with him on this subject, I realized. If a god as mighty as my father wanted to prove himself against the strongest of all the Titans, I could not stop or change that.

I needed to try a different tactic with the King of the Gods.

"Will you not return to us, as our king? Please, father. Lead us as you once did. Why do you wish to release Titans and cause our world such strife?"

Zeus snorted. "This is not a plea that the God of War should be making, Ares. You are supposed to want strife, boy! You should seek chaos and destruction; these powers are all linked to your own." He sneered down at me, his gaze seeming to bore straight through my armor. "You are a shadow of your former self." His eyes flicked to Bella. My chest constricted, fear bolting through me. Bella was kneeling, frozen in place and her gaze fixed on Zeus. I couldn't tell if it was awe or fear in her eyes.

"She has nothing to do with this."

"Oh, Ares. I rather think that she does," he breathed, stepping toward her. "She is interesting." The gruffness had gone from his tone, replaced with a dangerously low rumble. The fear inside me clawed its way up my chest, into my throat.

The last thing I wanted was for Zeus to take issue with Bella. Even his brothers could not best him, there was no way I could not stop him from hurting her.

I moved between them, fast. "Only one of us could be immortal while the other lives. You need have no interest in her; she is connected only to me."

"There are many prophecies in this world, boy." Zeus' eyes stormed with purple electricity as he looked at me. "I was happy to take your power and let your mother find a way for you to restore it. You were no threat to me, or my plans, and I had hoped it would keep Hera occupied. But now... This woman can make you strong, Ares. She has the potential to change you into something so much greater than you are now. Something... powerful. I can feel it now that you two are together. I can't let that happen."

"You're wrong," I said, even though I knew the truth

of his words as he said them. Bella did make me better, stronger, more powerful. But not in a physical way. "Only one of us can be immortal at any one time, and that makes us weak. We are no threat to you." It went against every fibre of my being to deliberately portray myself as weak, and I had to force the words from my lips, but it was the only thing I could think of to keep Bella safe.

"No, Ares. If you learn to share this power properly... Your lack of immortality is exactly what will make you unstoppable."

Lethal sparks danced in his eyes as he looked between me and Bella, and I thought my heart might stop beating altogether as I dropped to my knees. I was out of options.

"I will not oppose you, father. We are no threat, I swear it."

"And you, girl?" Zeus looked at Bella. "Do you swear it too?"

She looked at me, then at the giant god in front of us. "Yes," she said.

There was a long pause before Zeus spoke. "I do not believe you. There is an indomitable spirit inside you, that can not be crushed."

"Father, please. If you ever loved me, leave her alone."

His foot stamped down hard on the planks as he barked a laugh. "Aphrodite, come here."

The goddess sauntered over to him, making sure to throw Bella an evil look as she did. "Yes, my Lord?"

"Am I correct in my understanding that in failing the Trials, you now own the God of War?"

"Technically, the Lords own the God of War," she purred. "But we have an understanding."

"Good." Zeus looked back to me. There was death in his eyes, clear as day.

I felt physically sick as I tried to flash. I had already known it wouldn't work on this ship, but I had to try something. My mind raced, frantic to come up with a way to save her. "You know how I feel about murdering family members myself," said Zeus. "And your mother would never forgive me. So I'm afraid my only option is to kill the girl."

"No!" I leaped to my feet, only to be held in place by his magic.

"My Lord, may I interrupt?" Aphrodite's voice was silky sweet as I struggled against my invisible bonds. "If you kill the girl, Ares will get all of her power."

"You make a good point, Aphrodite. Let me fix that."

A bolt of lightning screeched down into the deck in front of Bella and she scrambled backward. I tried harder to move, barely able to breathe, but the lightning expanded, electricity shocking my skin as the tendril of purple power reached me. I heard the roar of pain ripped from my throat at the same time as I heard Bella's shout.

I tried to speak, to reach her, but I was pinned in place by the lightning, my whole body shaking as electricity tore through it.

"I would say I'm sorry, but it is what you deserve for crossing me, son," I heard Zeus say.

With a surge of power, the electricity reached my gut, and the connection to Bella. There was an agonizing tearing feeling, then the electricity stopped, draining away fast. And with it, my access to Bella's power.

31

BELLA

"No, no, no."

When the pain of the purple electricity ebbed away, I knew instantly that something was wrong. I could still feel Ares in my heart, but the connection we shared my power through... It was gone. An indescribably hollow feeling was left in its place, as though my body knew something was supposed to be there, but didn't know what.

"Don't kill her!" Ares' voice was ragged and I longed to reach for his hand, but I was being held where I was by a magic that I knew I could never best. As I thought about the strength of my power, a rushing feeling started, like when Dentro had flown me away from Ares in the forest, but more.

Healing magic flooded through my body like a raging river, washing away every trace of fatigue and pain from every cell. I felt like my muscles were growing, hardening, filling with strength.

My power was returning to me, no longer able to

reach Ares at all. And... And there was something else. Something new. I probed inside myself, trying to work out what the dark, creeping feeling was.

Terror.

Recognition dawned on me. It was Terror's power. It must have returned to Ares when we shattered his mortal body. And now it was flowing into me.

Zeus stepped forward, and the addition of Terror's power to my own receded abruptly in importance. I summoned a fireball, projecting it directly from my chest as hard as I could, aiming for the giant before me.

It sizzled out before it got a foot away from me. The mass of power pinning me in place thickened, preventing me from moving and squeezing me tight.

Zeus, King of the Gods and all-powerful deity, wanted me dead. And all the spirit and fight in the world couldn't save me from him. Nor could Ares.

"I love you," I said, unable to turn my head, but sure he would know I was talking to him. "Whatever they do to us, I will never regret finding you."

"Bella, don't give up."

"Never," I said. "I just wanted you to know that." I expected my heart to be racing, my stomach to be filled with butterflies, fear to be consuming me. But a weird calm had come over me.

If I was going down, there was one god I was taking down with me.

"I love you too." A spear of emotion accompanied his words, and a sorrow that I would not get to feel his touch, or kiss his lips, or hear his voice for a long and happy life welled up inside me.

It's not over yet.

"Have you finished your goodbyes?" Zeus boomed, and I took a deep breath.

"I've died a hundred times over," I said, as loudly as I could. "What's one more death?"

The massive god cocked his head at me. "I understand your fondness for her," he said to Ares.

"Please, father," he rasped.

It was all the distraction I needed. A fireball three times the size of the first one burst from my chest. But I wasn't aiming for Zeus this time.

It smashed into Aphrodite before she even realized it was coming, such was the speed of my fully returned power. Shrieking filled the air as her dress caught fire. Zeus snapped his fingers, my raging inferno doused instantly.

"You should be paying more attention, Aphrodite," he chided her. I saw that the skin of her beautiful face was charred and blistered, before it began to knit back together. But it didn't disguise the fury.

"It is time for her to die," she growled, a black dress wrapping around her body out of nowhere, to replace the one I'd just burned to ash.

"Indeed." Thunder rolled and lightning flashed.

Teal lightning.

I saw confusion cross Zeus' massive face for a split second, before Hera shimmered into being on the deck of the ship. She was as large as Zeus, and the rage on her face rivaled Aphrodite's.

"You dare to interfere with bonds this ancient? You dare to ruin our son's life?" The goddess advanced on

Zeus, growing even larger. My own breath caught. She was magnificent, a powerhouse of dark skin and teal silks and an aura as intense as Zeus'. I wanted to *be* Hera in that moment. "I have been spending every drop of energy I possess keeping you from your own idiocy these last months, but now you have pushed me too far!"

Zeus' eyes darkened as he glared back at his wife. "You do not know what you are preventing me from doing. Release your hold on me and let me get on with rebuilding our world."

Hera gave a humorless laugh. "Zeus, I am the only Olympian who has any control over you. That's what my bonds do. They connect two people. I am as bound to you as you are to me. I will not let you make these mistakes. And I will not let you kill a part of our son's soul."

"That girl could be the downfall of us," Zeus hissed.

"I do not care. You have gone too far."

They were nose-to-nose now, and I was holding my breath watching them. My leg twitched where my knee met the hard planks, and I realized that I could move again. I turned my head, ever so slowly, drinking in the sight of Ares a few feet away.

"Wife, leave me!" Zeus roared.

"Not this time, husband," Hera replied, and fast as lightning she gripped his face in her hands. There was a loud crack, a flash of purple and teal light, and they were gone.

. . .

I fell forward onto my hands as the remnants of power holding me in place vanished with them. Strength pulsed through my whole body, and I was on my feet in seconds. Nobody would have known that just hours ago the wound in my thigh had been bordering on killing me. I felt fucking invincible.

Aphrodite was staring at the space Zeus had occupied a second ago and rage took me in its grip, instinct and power taking over. I still could feel magic filling me, as though my body was its refuge now that it could not reach Ares.

"What are you going to do now that he's gone, Aphrodite?" I hissed, and my voice didn't sound like my own.

"I don't need Zeus to fight my battles," she said, though I could see the uncertainty in her eyes. "Pain! Panic!" she called.

"Ahhh, so you need some folk with the power of War instead," I said, narrowing my eyes. I knew they would be blazing. I could feel the heat rolling from me as my body began to swell, accommodating the massive energy churning through my limbs. "Because you're too pathetic to fight me."

"I am not so crude as to fight with my fists."

"No. You fight with cruel words and unkind manipulations," Ares said before I could answer. He was on his feet, and though he was large and solid in his armor, he had no glow, no aura of power around him. I met his eyes briefly, and projected as much love and confidence as I could into my gaze. I felt the bond between our souls fire, and knew he'd got my message.

We would work out how to get his power back as soon as we could, but right now we had a war to win.

Together, we stepped toward Aphrodite, as the Lords moved to her side.

"I do not need to fight you at all," she spat. "Not when I have a small army to do it for me."

She held her hands out and they glowed brightly. "You have been summoned, ugly one," she called loudly.

Cold descended over the ship as shadows started to crawl over the deck. I recognized the feeling at once. It was the Underworld demon.

32

BELLA

The Lords spread out on either side of Aphrodite, cruel grins distorting their handsome faces.

I scanned the darkening skies quickly for Dentro, but the dragon was nowhere to be seen. The temperature dropped further and the light from the sails dimmed as the shadows stretched.

I knew what was coming.

Lifting my hand at the same time as Aphrodite lowered hers, I threw up a dome around Ares. Physically, he was strong as hell, but he was powerless against the Lords, Aphrodite and the demon. The thought of him losing his soul caused a new wave of roiling anger to wash through me.

Pain advanced suddenly, and I became aware of a sensation sparking up my legs from the planks. It didn't take long for the sensation to worsen, and pain to start causing my still growing muscles to spasm. I used my magic to force the feeling away, and only realized when Ares growled in pain that the shield I had put around him was under attack, Pain's magic able to get to him through it.

I poured more power into the shield, but as soon as I did, the pain in my own body returned, hard enough to make one knee buckle.

I heard Aphrodite laugh as I clenched my jaw against the growing agony.

"Your turn, Panic," she cooed.

Instantly, the shadows lengthened, and the memory of my last encounter with the Keres demon sprang into my mind. *You can't defeat her. Swords don't work, strength doesn't work, fire doesn't work. You can't defeat her, useless little goddess.*

The voice sang in my mind, allowing the panic to siphon my confidence, allowing it to poison my power as it flowed through my veins.

I felt the shield weaken as the waves of agony grew, and my other leg buckled.

"Leave the shield, fight them," choked out Ares.

"I can't! What if the demon comes? I won't risk losing your soul."

"You can't defend me and fight, Bella. And you must fight."

A loud, feline snarl made me turn, and my breath caught as Zeeva leaped out of the door from the closest quarterdeck. She was huge and lethal looking in her sphinx form, moving with an unearthly grace. I had never been happier to see her.

Even better, she was holding my helmet and sword in her massive mouth.

"Zeeva, you're a fucking legend," I breathed as she tossed her head as she ran, sending them skittering across the planks toward me. I reached out, stopping the helmet with my knee and scooping up *Ischyros*. Heat rushed into my palm as the sword hummed happily.

"I know," the cat answered, then launched herself at Pain.

The Lord shrieked as she made contact with him, and the agony causing my legs to fail me vanished. Aphrodite stumbled backward, out of the way of Zeeva as she hissed and snarled, slashing with her huge paw at Pain.

I jumped back to my feet, then Ares was up too, running toward me.

Our hands caught each others, fingers entwining as he smashed his lips into mine. For the briefest second of bliss, the fight vanished in the joy of a moment I feared I would never experience again. But he pulled away too soon.

"Bella, you must fight, whatever happens to me. You have all the power now, and you are at full strength. You are a true goddess. You can win."

"I won't let them hurt you."

"Let the power take over, Bella. Embrace who you really are. You're the Titan Enyo, Goddess of War."

"I don't know who that is. I don't even know who I

am anymore if I don't have you." I could feel my fear of the demon spreading over me, clouding my thoughts. "I can't lose your soul. I don't know how to stop her, she's not made of flesh and bone."

"Then don't become Enyo." Ares cupped my face in his palm and I heard Aphrodite scream for the demon again. "Become *Bella*, Goddess of War. You have all of your power. You have the ability within you to command the Lords of War. You heard what Zeus said. He feared you, Bella, the King of the Gods himself. You are mighty and powerful. You will win."

Icy cold blew across the deck as his words smashed through the wall of doubt that had been erected between me and the almost overflowing power inside me.

I was powerful. I knew that much was true, the rage inside me was becoming hard to contain, a tornado of brutal energy.

An awful high-pitched wail floated over us, making me want to cover my ears. Instead, I pressed my lips hard to Ares', then stepped back and lifted my helmet. Taking a deep breath, I slid it down over my head.

I raised *Ischyros*.

I will win. Ares believed it. And now I needed to.

I had to embrace who I was. I had to become the Goddess of War. But not Enyo. I had no use for an ancient version of myself I had never known. I needed to be what I had made myself, the same woman who had come back from every shitty existence stronger. The same woman Ares had fallen in love with.

I felt my spine straighten, and my blood run hotter in my veins.

I was Bella, and I was a fucking goddess.

33

BELLA

The Keres demon burst onto the deck in a wave of black smoke so thick I could barely see though it. The Lords and Aphrodite disappeared in the haze, as the smell of blood and rotten flesh overwhelmed my nostrils.

"You came back, sweet-smelling one. And now your scent is even stronger."

The demon's voice made every hair on my body stand on end, like nails over a chalkboard.

"I'm here to send you back to hell," I snarled, raising my sword. "I am fucking sick of batshit-crazy goddesses and soul-sucking demons trying to hurt the people I love. This ends now."

I gripped the hilt of my sword with both hands and held it high, just as I had seen myself do on horseback in the visions of me in the purple dress.

Like the long lost pieces of a puzzle flying back into place, the vision suddenly made sense. I knew exactly what I was seeing as I closed my eyes and let it wash over me completely. The smell of the grassy earth, the roar of my army's battle chant, the beating of the drums, the sound of hooves pounding the ground.

It was one of my previous lives. One where I had won the most glorious honor of them all. One where I was fierce and strong and wise and I led my people to victory.

Ares was right. I could command the power of War. I was *born* to command the power of War.

When I opened my eyes, gold light was pouring from my body in rivers, and a thrill like I had never felt filled me as I watched. The army from my vision, hundreds of well-muscled men and women on horseback barely half-a-foot in height, were galloping along the beams of light, their swords and axes raised aloft like mine. The demon wailed as the light reached her and began to wrap around her grotesque form as though it were a lasso, ridden by an endless wave of warriors. The air was filled with the sound of the army's battle chant and the thudding of hooves.

I gave my own battle cry as power flowed from my center, the light continuing to pour from my chest and the fearless riders tearing their way toward their enemy, growing in size as they reached her. Within moments there was a tornado of golden light whirling around the demon, and I caught flashes of weapons and horse heads and painted faces amongst the gold as they galloped around her, the drum beats echoing loudly.

.   .   .

Something slammed into me and I staggered.

"Zeeva!" It was the sphinx that had hit me, and whilst I had managed to stay on my feet, she had slid across the planks. She had her teeth bared, a terrible hissing sound coming from her as she jumped back up.

"That Lord will die!" she screamed, and before I could say another thing she had pounced back into the billowing smoke that was covering the deck like fog.

"Bella, she has my power!"

Ares' voice rang in my head, and I closed my eyes, focusing.

The demon had Ares power. I had to get it back. "Your power is gone, pathetic little pup." Aphrodite stalked through the smoke, glowing fuchsia. But she was lying. Ares' power was there, I could feel it emanating from the demon. Why wasn't she using it?

Summoning every drop of concentration I could, I launched myself into the dark space Ares had taught me to access when I sought out Hippolyta via her War magic.

Everything stilled as I found myself in the inky nothingness, a blazing column of red and gold light directly before me, ringed by my mounted army. The bright, shimmering forms of Pain and Panic were there too, as well as a number of less bright lights in the distance, but they were all eclipsed by the beacon of Ares' power, contained inside the demon.

"Keres demon! Release the War power, now! Give it back to its rightful owner!" I shouted the words with no real hope that they would have any effect. I didn't have the first clue how to get Ares power back. All I knew was that I needed to do something and I couldn't kill the demon.

Or could I?

The question burst, unbidden, into my head, and it took me a second to realize that it wasn't my own. It was Terror's voice.

You can kill her. Zeus said you were powerful enough to be a threat. Of course you can kill one demon.

"Why would I help you?" The demon's awful voice emanated from the beam of Ares' power. I forced more of my own power into the swirling ring of light.

"It is not your power to bear."

"As well I know." Her voice was bitter, and everything I knew about power in Olympus whizzed through my head. Ares gave power to hosts, like the Lords, to use. But *he* hadn't given the demon this power, someone else had.

"You can't use the War magic, can you?"

"I do not need it. My own is plenty."

"Then you won't mind if I take it back."

I pulled on my bond to Ares, filling my every cell with him, calling his soul to mine. His power was a part of his soul, he had said. And though the connection in my gut was gone, the one in my heart was as strong as ever.

Slowly at first, the beam of light flickered. Then with a sear of heat it began to rush toward me, along my own golden river of light.

I opened my eyes and gripped Ares' hand, at the same time that the demon wailed. He jerked beside me, then his eyes widened as his power began to flow into him through me.

"Stop!" screamed Aphrodite, rushing toward us.

But she was too late. Like a long-lost dog eager to return to its master, Ares' power had rushed to him in a mere heartbeat.

Gold burst from him as he grew, his own river of light pouring from his gleaming armor and smashing into Aphrodite. The army that raced along his light was made up of footmen with helmets like his own, massive Greek shields and lethal spears. The chants of battle and screams of death echoed through the air, and I felt my own army respond, galloping faster on their horses.

"Ares! Ares, release me!" Aphrodite was screaming as the golden warriors surrounded her, whipping into a tornado just like my own and trapping her.

Strength surged inside me as Ares' eyes locked on mine, flaming.

"We can kill her," I said, before I knew I'd even thought the words. "Both of them. We're strong enough together, I can feel it."

"No, Bella. Hades and Poseidon need to deal with this."

But burning fury was rolling through me, needing to be expelled. "She tried to kill you. She tried to keep us apart."

The golden light running from me was tinged red. It looked a little like fire. I cocked my head at it.

"They need to burn," I said. My head was swimming with images of Aphrodite succumbing to flames, her face a mask of fear, her voice a cowering plea.

"Bella, that's Terror's power talking. Not yours."

"Ares, I want her dead."

"I'll leave!" Aphrodite's voice rang out from inside her cage of light. Her face was just visible through the spinning gold. "You'll never see me again, I swear. Just let me go."

"Lies." I stepped toward her, my light turning completely red. The demon let out a choked wail, but I barely heard it. "You lie, little goddess," I spat. "Demon! You can take souls, yes?" I didn't take my eyes off Aphrodite's, now filling with the fear I was so desperate to see. I could feel the power of Terror's thrill at her reaction. And I embraced it. I couldn't help it. This woman had tried to take everything from me. I had done her no wrong.

She had treated Ares like a fucking toy.

"Yes," rasped the demon.

"Can you take the soul of an immortal?"

"No. But... I can take power."

Glee sparked inside me. "Take her power."

"No!" Aphrodite shrieked.

"Bella, this is not you. This is Terror's influence." Ares' voice was calm, his eyes still blazing as he turned me to face him.

"She deserves to suffer as you have."

"I agree, but we should not be the ones to dole out punishment."

"Listen to him! He is wise," Aphrodite choked. Ares' eyes flashed dark as he turned to her.

"You have spent centuries calling me a fool,

Aphrodite. I do not plea for mercy on your behalf because you deserve it."

"Then why? Why do you want to show her mercy?" I could hear the jealousy in my voice. I felt my body swell as even more anger poured through me. I had to fight. I had to win. I had to prove what I was capable of.

"Because you have taught me the importance of fairness."

"It is fair that she suffers as you have!"

Ares' jaw twitched. "Perhaps. But you have Terror's cruelty inside you now. Do not act on his will."

"It is my own will that wants to see her pay."

Ares opened his mouth to answer when agony ripped through my spine. I cried out as I dropped to the planks, and Ares rushed to catch me. I felt my river of light cut off, then heard Pain's voice as I doubled over.

"Flash us away, Aphrodite, now!"

"No!" I straightened in Ares' arms, desperate to stop Aphrodite escaping, but froze at what I saw.

The Keres demon had reached Aphrodite before she could flash away. My stomach churned, bile rising in my throat as the rotten corpse-like form towered over the beautiful goddess, pink light pouring from Aphrodite's chest into the gaping mouth of the demon.

Pain made a strangled sound, but I couldn't take my eyes off the horrific scene in front of me. I clung to Ares, and he gripped me hard back. A sense of utter wrongness spread through me, the idea of my own power being leeched from me like that unbearable.

A true understanding of what it must have been like for Ares to have his power stolen settled over me.

"You... you were right. This wasn't what I wanted. It feels so wrong."

Ares was silent a moment before answering, his voice grim. "I was going to say the opposite. I think it is exactly what she deserves. I just didn't want you to be forced into doing something by Terror that you would regret."

The demon turned to us suddenly, and Aphrodite slumped to the deck. A sob bubbled out of her.

"I have done as you bid, new mistress. Will you now let me leave?" The demon's voice made me feel even more sick, the headache returning instantly. Dark smoke billowed around us. Aphrodite's sobs got louder.

"Keres demon! You will return with me now!" The voice blasted across the deck, along with a freezing wave of air that made my body want to shrink and hide. With an almost blinding flash of bright blue light, Hades appeared on the deck.

The thick smoke dissipated, but I was too transfixed on Hades to notice anything else. The blue light that had accompanied the God of the Dead was solidifying into people, just like mine and Ares' had. In a rush, they swarmed the demon.

"Mistress! Mistress, help me!" the demon screamed, and I realized with another lurch of my stomach that she meant me.

There was a loud crack, another bright flash of blue, and Hades and the demon vanished.

The sky brightened immediately, the solar sails

casting a warm glow over everything as they refilled with light.

"How..." I stared around, my mind thick with oncoming fatigue and confusion.

"I called him and Poseidon," Ares said gently, and I realized with a start that the God of the Sea was standing over Aphrodite's crumpled form.

"You can't beat Zeus, Poseidon. He is stronger than you and Hades combined," she said through tears.

I scanned the deck. Pain was laying down, covered in blood, with Zeeva crouched over him, still in sphinx form. Panic was cowered against the main mast.

"If you are in league with my brother, Aphrodite, then you are at war with us." Poseidon's voice was low and grave.

"I have made my choice, fool. It is the right choice." I had to admit that there was courage to Aphrodite's words. A courage I had previously not credited her with.

"Then you leave me no choice." The manacles appeared in the sea god's hands, and a bolt of satisfaction tore through me as Aphrodite blanched, the manacles magically snapping into place on her delicate wrists.

"Thank you, Enyo," Poseidon said, before they both vanished in his own flash of aqua-blue.

"It's Bella." I whispered.

34

BELLA

"**P**ain, Panic, recognize me now as your creator and master. Kneel," Ares barked. Panic knelt at once, fear in his face. Pain struggled to a kneeling position, but Zeeva swiped with her paw as soon as he was upright, sending him slumping back to the planks with a grunt.

"Sorry. I couldn't help it," she said.

Ares gave her a look, then spoke again. "Return to your realms and await my judgment. You will suffer for your mutiny. If you even consider defying me, you will die."

"Yes, master." Both men flashed and I didn't blame them. I'd be getting out of there as fast as I could too. Ares cupped my cheek again, and I drank in the emotion on his face.

"You were amazing," he said.

"So were you. I... I'm sorry I went a bit..." I trailed off.

"When I first had to manage Terror's power it was hard. You did better than I did."

"Really?"

"Yes. Bella, I really thought I was going to lose you. More than once." Gently, he lifted the helmet from my head, followed by his own. He lowered his head, his beautiful, serious face inches from mine. "I love you." His lips met mine, and it was the most tender kiss we had ever shared. The fire and drums and heat were simmering under a passion that went a million times further than my physical desire for him.

I pressed myself into him, winding my fingers around his neck and kissing him deeper.

"I love you," I told him mentally. *"I could never lose you."*

He moved back, holding my face in both of his hands, a pained look in his eyes. "I'm sorry. I'm so, so sorry about what I put you through."

"Let's not talk about it. It's done."

"I... I misunderstood the prophecy. I thought that to be immortal, you must not exist. But now, I would take you over immortality in a heartbeat."

"Well, now that you have your power back, you don't need to make that choice."

His expression darkened, and I knew why before he spoke. "I felt alive when I shared my mortality with you."

"I know. I don't really want this either. But it is better than one of us having to live without the other."

"That is true."

I stood on my tiptoes, kissing him again.

"What will happen to them?" I asked, when I pulled away.

"Aphrodite will be a prisoner and the demon will be returned to Hades' care."

"Not going to lie, I quite like the thought of her a prisoner. But what about her power?"

Ares shrugged, the metal of his armor moving against me. I glanced down, noticing that we were both still glowing. "I'm sure Poseidon will make the right decision."

"And the souls that the Keres demon took?"

"Hades will keep his promise to return them, I am sure."

I nodded, relief taking me under like a wave. It was over. No more Trials, Joshua would be safe, and most important of all, Ares and I were together.

"Ares, can we go home now?"

"Of course. I think I would like some of that silly drink you like so much. What is it called again?"

"Tequila," I beamed at him.

"Yes. Tequila."

"Can we drink it naked?"

"I wouldn't have it any other way."

"I am sorry to interrupt," a deep voice said. The scent of the ocean wafted over me as I turned in unison with Ares.

"Oceanus," he breathed, and we both bowed to the ancient Titan as he appeared to walk straight out of the brilliant solar sails and down to the deck, as though he were on an invisible staircase.

"It appears that you have completed your task," he rumbled. He was wearing a worn looking toga, no shoes, and his grey hair was tied back from his tanned face. Once again, he looked nothing like I expected the most powerful god in Olympus to look. He looked a like a hot older fisherman at a toga party.

"My power is returned, Oceanus. I am no longer in need of your offer of a Trident."

Oceanus' blue eyes sparkled. "I have been impressed with your commitment to proving yourself a worthy god, Ares."

He stiffened beside me. "Thank you," he muttered.

"Is there something else I can offer you, in place of the Trident?"

Excitement skittered through me, and when Ares looked at me, I knew he was thinking he same thing.

"The connection that Zeus destroyed," I said, my face splitting into a smile.

Oceanus cocked his head. "The one that allowed you to share your power? That made you both mortal?"

"Yes. That one," Ares nodded. "Can you restore it?"

"Yes, but... that would mean removing the power you just won back. Is that really what you're asking me to do?"

Ares gripped my hand, turning me to face him. "Bella, are you sure you want to share power again? We can be immortal for eternity like this, both true gods with the full strength of Olympians."

"I don't want to be immortal for eternity! I want to

live my life like it means something, sharing every experience with you." And it was true. The longer we had spent together, the more I had come to love sharing my power with Ares. The tugging feeling in my gut, the way he poured healing power into me when I needed it... It was just so right, somehow.

"So do I. I don't want the life I had before you. I want what you have opened my eyes to. I want to learn what all these ridiculous emotions do, and feel the thrill of taking risks." His eyes danced with excitement as he talked.

"Then the decision is made," I beamed at him.

My stomach was turning somersaults as we turned back to Oceanus.

"We would like to share the power of one god again. It does not matter whether it is mine or Bella's. As long as it is like it was before."

Oceanus' wise face relaxed into a smile. "Your decision pleases me. I would like to offer you both a gift."

A small bracelet appeared on my wrist, and Ares held his arm out, a matching one on his much larger arm. They were made of twine, and had three tiny seapearls threaded onto the band.

"These will not make you immortal but they will stop you aging. Olympus needs a God or Goddess of War; we can't have you going and dying on us in fifty years."

I looked between the bracelet and Oceanus. "So we will live forever as long as we are not killed in battle?"

"Yes. You can still be killed by anything except old age."

"Thank you," Ares said, sincerity bordering on reverence in his voice.

Oceanus chuckled. "Never have I heard such gratitude for the gift of being able to be killed." He shook his head.

With a whip of his hand I felt a warm tingle spread through my stomach, then a laugh escaped my lips as I felt the connection snap back into place. Ares pulled me to him, kissing me happily as the waves of energy rolling through me lessened, the well of heat under my ribs shrinking. Then I felt the familiar tug as what remained of our power moved between us, leveling out.

Our power. Not mine, not Ares'. Ours.

35

BELLA

"I wish you hadn't made me come here," Ares grumbled. I rolled my eyes but didn't turn to look at him.

"You know exactly why you're here. Because I don't trust myself to flash all the way to the mortal world yet."

"Well, hurry up. The announcement about the fighting pits is soon."

Ares was sulking because I had insisted on seeing that Joshua was safe with my own eyes. The truth was, I wanted him here because I knew he harbored some jealousy over my old crush and I thought he'd worry less if he was here too.

I watched Joshua through the window of his office, disguised from view by my shield. He was talking animatedly to a patient, and as far as I was aware, he had no idea I was anywhere near him. Or even that I existed at all, let alone that I had saved his soul.

Hades had kept his word, returning all the souls that the demon had stolen. Many of the mortal hosts had been killed, but Hades' right-hand woman, Hecate, had worked some sort of magic to help recreate them, and a god called Hypnos, who also worked for Hades, had helped reset their loved ones memories. I was hazy on the details, but Persephone had assured me that my concerns about zombies were unfounded. It was something to do with creating new bodies, and reinserting the souls, with all their own memories. Joshua was still Joshua, just in a brand new body that looked like the old one.

The power the gods had over the world I had called my home was slightly overwhelming, but I had a long time to get used to it. Forever, if I didn't manage to get myself killed.

"I'm done. I just wanted to check I'd achieved what I set out to do," I said, turning to Ares. "Which was save my friend." I emphasized friend but he still scowled at me.

"The way I remember it, you set out to annoy me."

"Then it appears I have achieved twice today."

He gave me a look, then pulled me close to him, brushing my hair out of my face as he stared down at me. "You can annoy me every day for eternity, if it makes you happy," he said softly.

"Then I shall," I grinned back at him. "But right now, we have to go. Your announcement is coming up."

. . .

Ares flashed us back of the deck of his ship, and I half-skipped to the railings. We were hovering right over the center of the largest fighting pit in his realm. People were starting to fill the rows of seats, and excitement trickled through me.

Ares had needed to take care of a whole load of issues after the Trials. First and foremost was finding Eris, but we'd come up blank. While Hades was fixing the damage the demon had done and restoring the Guardians, we had combed every inch of the mortal realm with Persephone's help. But we couldn't find a single trace of the Goddess of Chaos. All we could do was hope Poseidon would be successful at getting Aphrodite to tell us what she had done.

Reluctantly, Ares had moved onto fixing his own realm. And that meant finding a new host for Terror. I'd met all the candidates with him, and Ares made sure I had a say in the final decision. I didn't trust the harpy-hybrid we had chosen one little bit, but I was confident she would be able to keep the spirit of Terror in check for a while at least.

Now, Ares had to prove to his realm that he was still as strong and as mighty as the God who had ruled them for centuries, and that he was still deserving of their respect.

And I had convinced him that the best way to do that was a tour. Right after the announcement that he was due to make, we would be setting sail for a full circuit of his realm, and we would be stopping in every single kingdom, to prove just how strong and worthy of respect we were. I was so excited my head actually hurt when I thought too much about it.

"Good luck today, fierce one. I must return to my brethren now." I heard Dentro's voice in my head and scanned the skies above me. A tiny dot in the distance swooped in response.

"Thank you for everything, Dentro. Drop by any time."

"I am sorry I could not help on the ship."

"You brought Ares to me. That was everything I needed. You could not have done more to help me."

"Goodbye, for now, Bella."

"Bye, Dentro. Have fun."

I heard his chuckle as the dot in the distance disappeared from view.

My sadness that my dragon friend was leaving was tempered significantly by the fact that my cat friend had gone nowhere. Zeeva had been worried that she had broken Hera's strict rules when she shifted and practically saved my life on Aphrodite's ship, but she had gotten a message from her mistress shortly after. Hera had said nothing about where she and Zeus were, only that she had sent a message to Hades, and that Zeeva was released from her duties until Hera could return.

And to my delight, Zeeva had decided to stay with me, on Ares' ship. I knew she loved me really.

"Are you ready?" Ares asked me, as I emerged from the bedroom twenty minutes later.

I was wearing full armor, helmet and all, as was Ares. "Ready as fuck," I answered him. He shook his head, but his eyes were smiling behind the helmet.

"Good. Let's do this."

The ship sank low into the fighting pit as we made our way onto the deck, so that we were level with the now-packed spectator seats ringing the stadium. Together we swelled in size, only stopping when we were both twenty feet tall, and everyone in the pit could see us clearly. Silence met us and my stomach fizzed with anticipation.

"Citizens of my realm," boomed Ares, and the connection in my gut pulled as he drew power to magnify his voice. "From this day on, no man, woman or creature shall fight against their will in Aries."

Instantly, the crowd let out a collective buzz of surprise.

"Prizes for fighting will be large and rewarding, and only those who are willing can compete for them. The penalty for breaking this new law is death. Fight and be victorious!"

A cheer went up, quiet at first, but louder as it gathered momentum. The citizens of the most dangerous realm in Olympus were a special kind of people, brutal and hard and fierce. I couldn't wait to meet them. I beamed behind my helmet.

"Now, we tour Aries. We hope to see many of you on our travels. Good luck to you all."

The ship moved, lifting us fast into the clouds, and I

pulled my helmet from my head. Ares did the same. "Where do you want to go first?" he asked, fire dancing in his beautiful eyes, his skin glowing gold.

"Everywhere. But maybe we should start with the bedroom."

"I love you, my golden goddess."

"And I love you, my warrior god."

THE END

FOR NOW...

READ ON FOR THE EPILOGUE AND TO FIND OUT WHICH GOD'S STORY IS COMING NEXT

36

EPILOGUE

"**G**ive me my power back!" Aphrodite screamed from the other side of the grand wooden door.

I closed my eyes and took a deep breath. "No. Not until you tell us what Zeus is planning."

The truth was, I would love nothing more than to hand her cursed love power back to her. I eyed my trident with a scowl. Between us, Hades and I had managed to remove her power from the rogue demon and store it in my weapon. The weapon that was a literal part of my soul.

I was able to keep her power from affecting mine, but its constant tumultuous presence was a distraction I could do without.

"Fine. I'll tell you. Poseidon, open the door."

My brows jumped at her words. She was being held in a nice room in my own palace, but I knew she wouldn't last long without her power. She would relent and tell us what we needed to know.

But I hadn't expected her to cave so soon.

I opened the door to her room slowly.

Her eyes fixed on mine. Even without her power, she was beautiful. Her hair was a rich black, her skin pale as snow. Her eyes were red from crying and I suppressed a pang of guilt. She had put Ares and Bella through hell, all for entertainment. She was not to be trusted.

She lunged for the Trident before I could process what she was doing. Cursing myself for allowing myself to be distracted, I yanked the weapon back, but her small fist had closed around it.

"I curse you, petty god of the sea," she snarled, and fuchsia light exploded from the trident. I drew on my colossal power, wrenching the weapon away from her and slamming the door closed in her face.

"Aphrodite, you can't win this! Just stop fighting me and tell us what we want to know!" I bellowed through the door, unable to contain my temper. Freezing water rushed up from my feet, swirling around my body and slamming into the wood.

"You're too late, Poseidon! Why don't you go and see that pretty wife of yours?"

My heart seemed to thud to a complete halt in my chest. "If you have done anything to harm my wife-" I didn't finish the sentence, whirling and racing down the corridor, Aphrodite's laughs dwindling behind me.

If a single hair on Amphritite's head was out of place, I would murder the Goddess of Love with my bare fucking hands.

THE POSEIDON TRIALS WILL BE COMING YOUR WAY SOON...
In the meantime, if you like your fantasy romance spicy and
you're into hot Irish men with big wings, check out my
brand new series, Lucifer's Curse.
Read on for a note from the author.

THANKS FOR READING!

Thank you so much for reading The Golden God, I hope you enjoyed it! If so I would be eternally grateful for a review! They help so much; just click here and leave a couple words, and you'll make my day :)

Bella and Ares were so, so much fun to write, and they really did run the show with this series. I normally plot my stories quite carefully, but the more I wrote about these two, the more stuff started happening that I simply wasn't expecting. Like Dentro for example - he was never supposed to be in the story! It was a blast to go on this adventure with the sweary, volatile, loveable-at-heart gods of war and I really hope you enjoyed reading it as much as I enjoyed writing it :D

I have to thank my mum, my husband, and my editor - I really couldn't be doing the job I love without you -
THANK YOU.

And even more, I want to thank **you** for reading.

I honestly can't believe that I've just typed THE END on my thirteenth book, and that's because you guys are so amazing. Every single page you read allows me to write more and I'm so grateful.

And I promise to keep the stories coming!

xxxxx